"We don't know what's going on," Luis said, "but I don't think it's trauma. I see no signs of disease. With the way it only affects some people in a family, I don't believe this is contagious at all. Mind if I ask you a question?"

Both Bitanthrans shook their heads.

"What do you think is going on? What do people who live here, who've been watching this happen for years, think?"

Willis drew in a slow breath, and Luis saw tears standing in his eyes.

"Some of us are afraid it's poison, something to do with Bitan. It seems to be getting worse over time. Like we've been exposed too much, and we're passing it along to our children."

"Well, I can't rule anything out yet since we just got started. But your medical center here has tested for every-thing we know of, and off-world facilities have too. Nothing seems out of line with your bodies. Nothing seems to accumulate or get depleted over time."

"Except our kids' feelings," Myrtle said. She didn't look sad like Willis. She looked furious. "That's depleting, more and more every year."

# THE BECALMED

KARI KILGORE

# Chapter 1

Luis Ahmad had tried every anti-nausea drug in all the galaxy and every home remedy from a hundred AlliedSystems planets. And without fail, as soon as a sub-light transport smaller than a vast ore freighter decelerated for orbit, he was sweaty and shaking, huddled beside the nearest receptacle.

His own specialty of deep psych-hypnosis didn't work any better than transdermal herb infusions from Beta Handsos. He'd even entered orbit submerged in a buoyant vat of Jemushian violet nectar. He had to admit that he smelled wonderful after that, but he still felt awful.

For a man with a body so ill-suited for interstellar travel, Luis often wondered how he'd stumbled into a career demanding just that. He'd never quite given up hope that hibernation technology, and safety regulations, would eventually allow him to wake up on his destination planet rather than hours before braking. A guy had to hope.

One reason he'd taken an assignment so far from Earth, on the edge of the far-flung Abrams System, was passage on the biggest ore freighter in the TransGalactic fleet. His hypersleep recovery cabin onboard the *Bountyfield* resembled nothing more than a dull steel rectangle, with five empty bunks wedged in around the floor-level spot he'd assigned himself. A few grunts and groans when he got up and down were a small price to pay for less gut-twisting motion.

The bass rumble as the ship's braking engines kicked in were the cue to keep himself focused with sensations other than his belly. Stretched out on the rock-hard mattress with his eyes closed, he ran his fingertips across the nubby blanket on his neatly made bed, pointedly ignoring the unfortunate shade of green.

He held his other palm flat on the cold, ridged floor. A mouth full of plain old Earth-style mint candies didn't do much to settle his stomach, but the sharp chill in his throat and nostrils gave him something else to concentrate on.

His position as TransGalactic's head psych-officer, not to mention the absurd amount they were paying him for this assignment, gave Luis the choice of far more luxurious recovery staterooms on board. Even the most rugged freighter carried a few for VIPs, and the *Bountyfield* was hardly rugged.

Commissioned only ten years ago specifically to make runs to the vital Abrams System, the forward section of the kilometers-long freighter could pass for TransGalactic's corporate headquarters. Silks from the moons of Kayren, mood-sensing crystal lighting from Outer Rigia. The finest chefs from around the known civilized systems. All standing ready for hypersleep recovery, on-board meetings, whatever the elite demanded.

And unfortunately for Luis, the staterooms were close to those gourmet kitchens, the better to waft tempting aromas through circulated air. Most humans woke ravenous. Avoiding food, no matter how expertly prepared, until he was planetside worked far better for Luis.

He opened his eyes when the braking engines cut out, leaving only the sound of his own breathing. The worst was over as far as gastric upset, but he was better off staying right where he was. The small crew on a big ship would work like ants racing ahead of a flooding river preparing for space dock. All Luis and any other passengers could do was get in the way.

He sat up carefully in case the grav-dampers still needed to adjust and pulled on a black wool jacket to match his pants. Luis pressed his back against the smooth, steadying wall. No bored long-haul crews had scratched or decorated it yet. One perfect coat of shiny TransGalactic blue would eventually give way to patches and repairs.

An hour until dock. May as well refresh his memory about the case that brought him such a long way. And focus his attention anywhere but on movement he could neither see nor control.

Luis pulled a spherical holo-reader out of his small woven aluminum daypack. He held the reader cupped in his palm, then pressed three fingers into the top to activate the display. He'd resisted the feather-light device at first, preferring the flat touch screen reader he'd grown up with.

The versatility of the display and the simple beauty of the nearly transparent ball won him over in the end. He adjusted the height until what looked like solid paper sat the perfect distance from his eyes before letting the reader float in place.

If Luis had been in one of those posh corporate staterooms several levels above, he would have a sprawling view of Bitanthra by now. More surface water than Earth on a smaller planet resulted in a thick grey and white cloud cover.

Native plants remained primitive and mostly safe, though humans with spring allergies tended to suffer greatly on the surface. A young, blue-tinted star left all that water looking especially brilliant if the observers weren't dealing with watering eyes.

The truth was nothing in particular recommended Bitanthra until TransGalactic got the sparkling deep-green ore scattered all over the rocky surface into their research and development labs. Decades later, Luis and most other sentient creatures understood what Bitan did. Only a handful outside of TransGalactic personnel ever had a chance to actually touch any.

Even the smallest grains were too valuable to remain unused.

Luis shifted his display, changing from text to images almost lifelike enough to take the place of touch. An uncut stone turned slowly in mid-air, gleaming pine forest green interrupted by brilliant flashes of purple, red, and orange.

A fine specimen like this, the actual size not much larger than a grown man's thumbnail, was worth more than a thousand homes on Earth.

Two quick metallic raps pulled Luis out of wondering if he'd have a chance to touch a piece of Bitan. He pushed himself to his feet, only grunting a couple of times. He slipped the reader into his day pack and activated the pack's magnetic seal.

## Chapter 2

A TransGalactic escort, obviously dispatched from the staterooms judging by her perfectly pressed midnight blue pantsuit and gleaming gold buttons, waited in the corridor. She looked about thirty, but with people in this line of work spending so much time in hypersleep, Luis never guessed about such things.

He didn't guess about TransGalactic pairing her with him, either. There were no classes or official documents admitting to it, but anyone on long-term hypersleep duty understood the open secret. Luis matched well with men or women with reddish hair, blue or green eyes, and fair skin. Her warm smile made it clear his brown eyes and hair and easily tanned skin fit her preferences as well.

"Dr. Ahmad. I trust your recovery has been smooth."

"Smoother than usual. Please, call me Luis."

"As you wish, Luis. I'm Tegwin Fairbrooke. We're boarding the first shuttle, if you're ready?"

"Lead the way."

The utilitarian steel hallway was decorated only with stripes of paint along the floor. Luis wasn't sure what the black, red, or green paths led to. He'd been told to follow the TransGalactic blue, and Tegwin did the same. Several crew members rushing past them wore sturdy canvas coveralls in colors matching the floor, but he didn't have a chance to see if they followed their proper stripes.

"Your first time on Bitanthra?" Tegwin said.

"It is. I've heard it's lovely."

She shrugged, continuing her quick pace. "Definitely peaceful. I don't mind ten days or so, but I think I'd struggle on a long ore loading stop with nothing else to do."

"Aren't they loading this time? I thought we were here for forty days."

Tegwin stopped in front of a personnel tri-axis motivator. Luis didn't love the unpredictable motion of a tri-ax, but it was unavoidable on a ship this size.

"I'll have plenty to do, Luis. I'm your corporate and planetary liaison. We can always catch a smaller freighter out if you're finished early, but the *Bountyfield* will be here for the duration. Before you ask, I trained in psych before I signed on with TransGalactic. Never had a chance to work much with hypnosis, though."

She waved her wrist in front of a round black sensor beside the tri-ax door. Luis hadn't noticed the thin silver com-bracelet she wore. He wondered how much Bitan it held, and how much a civilian would have to pay for one.

"You'll get plenty of chances to watch deep psych-hypnosis in practice if all goes well," he said.

The lift had the same boxy design as his recovery cabin had, with unpainted steel walls and a textured floor. Tegwin didn't do anything he saw, but the tri-ax moved smoothly to their right, toward the front of the freighter.

Most people swore they couldn't feel the damped motion and were surprised to find out where they ended up. Luis always knew.

"The shuttle will have us on the ground in about twenty minutes. Do you need medication for the drop?"

Luis laughed. "I see my reputation got here first. I'm usually fine as long as I can see and the shuttle isn't bumpy, thank you."

"You'll be able to see. Maybe better than you want to."

The tri-ax door slid to the side, and the reality of a working ore freighter slammed into Luis's senses. Whirring machinery, the stink of hot gears and human bodies working at top speed, a blur of people and material in motion. Tegwin stepped confidently into the controlled chaos, still following the blue stripe on the floor. Luis took a deep, mint-flavored breath, and followed.

When Luis spotted the curved bottom of the shuttle about a hundred meters away, Tegwin's comment made sense. The forward section was transparent, likely a proprietary TransGalactic alloy. The open cargo doors and the back of the shuttle were solid black, as shiny and new as the rest of the *Bountyfield*.

Luis followed Tegwin up a short flight of portable stairs into the crew seating area. White plastic seats with the thinnest of blue cushions were jammed in three to a side, with only a long, narrow window at shoulder height breaking up the matching white walls.

"You're welcome to stay back here if you think the drop will bother you," Tegwin said. "SteelGlas is every bit as strong as the rest of the ship, but some people prefer an enclosed space."

"I'd like to get a look at Bitanthra on the way down. If I have trouble, I promise I'll let you know before it's too late."

A wave of her wrist-comm, and they passed into another world. An absurdly expensive world created by the magic of that green rock. A black-carpeted walkway ran down the middle of the forward lounge, but the rest of the floor, walls, and ceiling were nearly invisible. The empty chairs up here were more like upright cocoons, all facing toward the center aisle.

Thick TransGalactic blue padding adjusted itself to Luis's body when he sat at the front of the shuttle, creating an odd sensation of both security and floating.

"We drop in about a minute." Tegwin settled in beside him. "I can call the attendant if you'd like refreshments or food."

"No, thank you. Are we the only ones going?"

"For now. There's a board meeting on the *Bountyfield*, so the shuttle will be bringing Bitanthrans back up for that. Most of the execs will be outbound on a smaller freighter in a few days, meeting with another colony. If you want to face out for the drop, press the armrest with your right hand. Another press brings you back."

Luis did a quick internal check. Everything felt secure for the moment. He swung himself out into what looked like solid black empty space.

He heard a faint wavering alarm, probably about a thousand times louder in the cargo hold, ending with a solid thud that jarred the shuttle.

"Outer shuttle door," Tegwin said. She'd positioned her chair beside his. "Drop begins now."

A line of light below Luis's feet broke the darkness, letting in a flood of white and blue light. The light grew upward as the inner door rose over the thick clouds of Bitanthra.

The shuttle glided forward, clearing the sides and top. When Luis saw nothing but clear space and choppy clouds with occasional flashes of dark beneath, the shuttle dropped. Not abruptly like most older models, and not too sharply. Luis hardly noticed his stomach's slow roll.

"We're over the sea right now." Tegwin pointed to flashes

of dark blue beneath them. "We'll circle the equator then heard north to the eastern mountain ranges. Smoother entry that way."

"That's where the mines are?"

"The big ones, yes. A few are scattered across all the land masses, and we've recently discovered Bitan deposits in the seas. The highest quality ore is still in the highlands."

Luis wished he could pull up the image of flashing green Bitan again, but he'd never been comfortable reading in motion. The reddish sun was hidden behind the mass of the *Bountyfield*, so he could observe the one source of the most important ore in the galaxy without a trace of glare.

A handful of those stones allowed communication across so far unlimited distances, all in real time. Voices and data traveled hundreds or thousands of light years in an instant, while the fastest transport in any fleet would take years or longer to make the same trip. Rapid colonization and the rise of the AlliedSystems would have been impossible without Bitan.

Luis had started out on this journey to save the most vital, and valuable, human colony in the known galaxy three Earth years ago.

To say the collapse of Bitanthra could lead to the collapse of the AlliedSystems and the TransGalactic empire, if anyone were brave enough to speak those disturbing words out loud, would be no exaggeration.

The problem here wasn't dissatisfaction with the workers, not like cautionary tales of labor struggles of the distant past on Earth or anywhere else. Everyone involved knew mining, processing, and shipping Bitan was never going to be easy. The stones were too fragile and soft for heavy automation or careless handling. Hours were long under and above ground. But TransGalactic took care of their invaluable colony and the people who made it work.

Luis wasn't here for the families of the workers either, at least not the adults. Several generations had been born and raised on the surface, and people rarely wanted to leave.

The colony was under serious and growing threat because of their children.

# Chapter 3

For the last thirty Earth years, a handful of the first native Bitanthrans, the offspring of the original human workers, seemed typical when they were born. They were physically healthy, curious and energetic, and of normal intelligence.

But over the next few years, the children steadily withdrew from their families and the rest of the world. They simply had no interest in the emotional lives of themselves or anyone else.

"You've been briefed on my mission?" Luis said before he realized how it sounded. "I'm sorry. You probably know more than I do. This isn't exactly open information outside of TransGalactic."

"We've worked hard to keep it that way. I always wake early so I can monitor what's happened while we were out. Several groups of women have been taken off-world for their pregnancies and births. No difference. If either parent was born on Bitanthra, the children are far more likely to have the disorder."

"What's the percentage now?"

Tegwin stared down at a break in the clouds, a sparkling glimpse of the star reflecting off the vast sea.

"It's passed fifty percent now."

The twist in Luis's gut had nothing to do with movement. His last briefing, the day before he'd gone into hypersleep, had put the rate at thirty-seven percent.

"It's accelerating so fast. Any progress on diagnosis or treatments?"

"Nothing useful to report. No detected toxin or other signs of disease. No effective treatment." Tegwin sighed long and low. "They're perfectly healthy aside from the complete lack of emotion. They hardly ever dream, either. That was in my last report. The few they have are mild and calm. No nightmares, for kids or adults."

Medical treatments had all failed, as had the same kind of folk remedies Luis constantly tried for his space sickness. Typical psychiatric treatments and drugs had no effect.

No one said the words, at least to him, about deep psych-hypnosis as a last resort in this case. Luis suspected other than moving hundreds of native families permanently off-world and destroying the society they'd built, Bitanthrans and TransGalactic were running out of options.

"How are the groups of affected children holding up?" he said. "Still living in their own communities?"

"They're doing well under the circumstances. The adults all live together, and they raise several of the affected children now too. They can work in sorting or processing, anything that's not dangerous. They seem to lack fear, or maybe the survival instinct to work underground. They've taken to calling themselves The Becalmed."

"Like an old sailing ship when the wind dies." Luis couldn't help respecting the word choice. He understood the separate communities as well. Neither group would be likely to make sense of the other no matter how hard they tried. "Do they know we're coming? What we're going to try?"

"They know about routine medical examinations, and they've all had regular psych evaluations from the time they were born. The current co-leaders have agreed to participate. Everyone knows no one has ever lied under a deep psych field. Honestly, I believe without the capability for fear or suspicion, it never occurs to them to resist."

Luis raised his eyebrows and focused on the much closer planet. The shuttle was aiming for a larger break in the clouds, and he could see dark yellow sand with spots of flashing metal down there. The equatorial resort zone was all most visitors to Bitanthra ever saw. Mining zones were too important and valuable.

Too many leaders in too many parts of the galaxy had tried to create a docile and compliant force of workers. Even if their methods hadn't been so horrific, the thoughts of people willing to destroy themselves because they couldn't resist was.

"I hate to bring this up before we even land," he said. "But has TransG considered this may not work? Do they have a plan for what to do then?"

Tegwin shook her head slowly.

"They've considered it obsessively. Just like with the medical treatments, nothing useful to report. Nothing they've passed along to me, at least. They established a colony here because it *is* so remote. That's gotten better with faster transports and more colonies out here on the edge of nowhere, but it will never be an easy trip. Men and women doing hard work are a hell of a lot happier if they go home at the end of the day instead of once every few years."

"Getting the existing colony disbanded wouldn't be easy, either."

"Not at all. They've been here for several generations

now. They're not from Earth or Beta Zhir or any other planet. They're from Bitanthra. There's something about this place, too. I'm sure you've heard how the natives feel about it."

Luis nodded. "I know they don't like to leave."

"No, that's not it." Tegwin frowned. "They *don't* leave. Ever. The women were furious at having to go off-world for their pregnancies and births. Men didn't much like it either. It wasn't the separation, really. They did not want to leave. I think they would have literally fought it if they weren't so afraid of what's happening to their kids."

"I've heard they're a fierce bunch."

"That's a mild way to put it. I have an odd theory I've never mentioned to anyone else." She glanced over her shoulder. A dozen or so fabulous chairs still sat empty. "I've wondered if people who are from here, the ones who aren't affected, are even more emotional than usual. Maybe not taking on what The Becalmed never had, but adjusted upward somehow."

Tegwin turned to face Luis, cheeks red and eyes defiant.

"I don't see why not," he said. "Is that any more strange than over fifty percent of their children being born without emotion at all?"

She stared at him for several seconds, then her face relaxed into her warm smile.

"It's not, is it? Listen, we're about to pass through the lower atmosphere. The pilot aimed forth the clearest area she could, but it could get a little bumpy."

Luis unwrapped a green and white striped mint candy for himself, then offered one to Tegwin.

"I haven't seen one of these since my grandfather kept a bowl full." She smiled when she popped it into her mouth, but her eyes were sad. "That was what, sixty, seventy years ago? So hard to keep track with all this hypersleep."

"Impossible."

"About as likely as keeping track of a relationship or anything like a family. Outside of these assignments, I mean."

That was another benefit of the open secret of mission pairings. Not only did everyone know. Most appreciated the opportunity in the middle of an incredibly disjointed life.

## Chapter 4

The TransGalactic pilot was as good as her word, bringing the shuttle down with barely a shudder. Luis wished the clouds were a little lighter so he could see the mountains rising up all around them. Short, narrow valleys cut through soaring peaks covered in a dense canopy of trees in every shade of green he could imagine. Broad rivers wound through the larger valleys, many carrying wide barges he guessed were full of ore.

Their landing port sat in a wider valley, but the surrounding town couldn't have held more than ten thousand people. Stone and wooden buildings dominated, with none terribly large or tall. Electric personal transports were plentiful, but more people walked than drove.

Luis had visited many small, slow-paced settlements like this on leisure-heavy planets, or in remote areas of more industrial zones. Their brief flyover of Bitanthra with this being by far the largest settlement made it clear how sparse the population really was.

He turned to Tegwin, supervising the offloading of their

luggage. A miniature mountain of his black bags and her TransGalactic blue ones sat neatly arranged in the open door of a transport that could have seated ten people. He didn't see any other passengers waiting.

"How many people live here now, Tegwin?"

"About four hundred thousand residents, mostly human. The tourist zone can accommodate around a hundred thousand more, but I doubt they've ever been full. That's just a side industry, mainly set up for the miners and their families. Bitan provides all they need."

"Looks like it."

Unlike other remote resource extraction colonies Luis had visited, everyone he saw on the perfectly maintained concrete sidewalks wore clean clothes in like-new condition. Simple work clothes to be sure, with old-fashioned Earth blue cotton jeans and cotton shirts and jackets in primary colors. But nothing seemed tattered or stained.

People were pale but healthy looking, sturdy and strong. The air itself was a thousand times cleaner than any other extraction colony as well. Instead of acrid dust or choking smoke, Luis smelled faint wood smoke, trees a bit spicier than Earth pines, and rich cooking smells from close by.

Now that he was on solid ground, his stomach reminded Luis that he hadn't eaten solid food for more than three years. Loudly.

"We're meeting the Bitanthran leadership in a couple of minutes." Tegwin said, her eyes merry. "They'll feed you until you beg for mercy. The Becalmed leaders will be there as well."

"Since they know you…"

"I know the older couple, yes. They've been briefed on the basics, but we'll explain deep psych in as much depth as they want. Or you will, anyway. That technology has advanced too much since I had my basic psych training for me to explain it. You're on your own with the food, though."

"I'll take that challenge."

# Chapter 5

Luis lost that challenge, giving up after his third plateful of food remarkably like that of old Earth. Like Tegwin, he remembered grandparents a hundred years older than his chronological years, along with their holiday customs and traditions.

Eager young Bitanthrans bustled Luis and Tegwin to a long wooden table covered with a heavy white tablecloth, then stuffed them full of potatoes, carrots, onions, and a lean meat they swore descended from Earth deer. A tall glass of milk from actual cows, not widely available anywhere besides Earth, nearly brought Luis to nostalgic tears.

The official delegation joining them for the meal was just as simple and reassuring. Two from each group, typical and Becalmed. Luis participated in the casual chat about weather, Bitan mining conditions, and polite questions about life off of Bitanthra.

He mostly watched the Becalmed man and woman watching the rest of them.

They looked no different from their counterparts at first glance. Same pale skin, sturdy build, and well-made work clothes. The Becalmed woman's black hair was as close cropped as the man's blond, whereas the typical woman wore hers long and pulled back from her face in glossy chestnut waves.

The most striking difference was Luis had no idea how old the Becalmed pair were. This wasn't the oddly fluid idea of age that years spent in hypersleep produced for himself and Tegwin. The Becalmed were clearly adult in face and body, lines of jaw and brow no longer soft with youth.

But those faces were smooth as a young teenager's, without a trace of lines around their eyes or mouths. The effect, along with the obvious understanding of every word even when they didn't speak, was eerie.

When everyone, meaning Luis, finally finished eating, Tegwin turned toward him.

"I know you understand the general idea of what Luis is here to do. He's the head psych-officer for TransGalactic, so he trains others on how to work with deep psych-hypnosis. He can explain a bit more and answer questions if you'd like."

Myrtle, the typical Bitanthran woman, nodded. Luis guessed she was in her fifties. While she did have lines on her face, she clearly smiled more than she frowned.

"We heard a lot about it over the last few months," she said. "While you two were inbound. I'd like to hear how you'd explain it, Luis."

"Tegwin's right, I've been on a few training assignments lately," Luis said. "So please stop me if I get too long-winded. You probably know hypnosis has been around for hundreds of years in one form or another. The difference with what deep psych can do is we map the brain first, so we get an idea of how your individual brain works."

"So you'll be able to tell why ours are Becalmed," Helen said. Her voice wasn't quite as flat and lifeless as an artificial life form, though it was lacking natural inflection. "Why our emotions are broken."

"I don't think brains are broken." Luis picked up his fork. "Not like a shovel or a fork can be. Each human brain, and mind, is unique. We store things in our own way, and the brain has amazing abilities to recover from traumatic injury. We don't know what's different about your brains yet. I hope we can figure that out."

"So you can fix us?" That was Drew, the Becalmed man. "Make us like everyone else."

Luis didn't miss the way Helen shook her head at Drew's words.

"I'm not going to force you to change anything you don't want to. We just want to figure it out. Get an idea why it's happening."

"If it happens to too many of the children," Myrtle said, her voice soft, "we won't have anyone left to mine Bitan. We may have to leave here."

Helen and Drew both nodded, but they showed no signs of being upset.

"That's the concern, yes," Luis said. "The main mission is to figure all of this out. Until then, I won't know if it's something that can be treated or changed. What deep psych allows me to do is pinpoint where an injury or disease lies in the brain, or where a traumatic memory is stored. Then we know where to target with our work instead of guessing."

"We don't believe there is any evidence of trauma." Tegwin touched Myrtle's shoulder. "Medical scans show no signs of disease, either. We're not sure what's going on yet."

Myrtle's partner Willis nodded. His hair was as dark as Luis's, but his beard was a deep red.

"So after you map the brain, you can do more with the hypnosis. Asking us questions and such. And we can't lie, right? Even if we wanted to."

"That's right. Especially with some traumatic memories, your mind tries to protect you and itself. Or the memory may be hard to access. The deep psych field allows us to get past those blocks and find out what's really going on. We're often able to free the blockage and relieve the trauma. Or in an injury or disease, help the brain find new pathways."

"Have you done that?" Drew said. "Has someone else hypnotized you, Luis?"

Everyone in the room, including Tegwin, turned toward Luis. He was used to students looking at him, but not all staring at once like that. He fought a giggle response involving baby birds out of his mind.

"Sure, several times during my own training. We were pioneering the technique, really, figuring out how to best use it to help people. All of us went under routinely. In groups many times, working together. I expect the next question is what is it like, and I'm sorry I can't answer. Not clearly. Most people don't remember much about their time under the deep psych field. All I remember is feeling relaxed after, like I'd had a good nap."

"How do we know what we told you?" Myrtle said, one eyebrow raised. "If we can't remember any of it?"

"We record the sessions," Luis said, with the same reassuring smile he always wore when answering that question. "The words as well as the data. Nothing is sent outside the room without your permission, not unless there *is* a crime. That's not what we're doing here. Once everything is finished, again with your permission, we delete all the words before I leave."

The four Bitanthrans looked each over for several seconds. Luis knew without asking Tegwin that he was under evaluation and the best thing he could do was stay quiet.

After a signal he didn't catch, Myrtle spoke. Her newly

formal words and manner carried the weight of ritual even in such humble surroundings.

"I am Myrtle, and this is Willis." She nodded to the red-bearded man beside her. "We are co-leaders of our people. We understand why you're here, Luis and Tegwin. We have great need of your help. With the consent of our Becalmed leaders, and if you are ready, we clear the way for you to begin your work."

"I am Helen, and this is Drew," the Becalmed woman said. "You have our consent to begin your work."

Luis froze, certain he was going to say something absurd and spoil his time here before it really got started. Tegwin saved him.

"I am Tegwin, and this is Luis. We appreciate your welcome, and your trust. We are ready to begin our work."

Luis managed to get to his feet an instant after everyone else did. He wasn't sure whether to be annoyed at himself for not asking about the protocol, or at Tegwin for not warning him. He hadn't expected to jump right in so soon after landing. But after years of sleep and with a comfortably stuffed belly, he couldn't think of a good reason to decline.

Not that any of the women in charge had asked him for one.

Tegwin followed the Becalmed pair out of the room, so Luis followed all three.

"We will go to the medical center," Helen said. "What will you do to get us ready for psych-hypnosis?"

Luis realized everyone was waiting for him to speak.

"It's painless, sometimes with a mild sedative. I believe the headgear should be waiting for us."

"It is," Tegwin said. "We have five private suites reserved. I thought we'd start with Helen and Drew. Myrtle and Willis have volunteered to act as a control group for typical Bitanthrans. They'll be here in a couple of hours. If we need other subjects, we'll go from there."

Drew held open a glass door set into a painted wooden building with Medical Center stenciled in white on the glass. Luis was pleasantly surprised to see what looked like a modern medical facility behind such a rustic façade.

A bright waiting room tiled in TransGalactic blue with gold accents, with nurses behind a sealed glass window. Even an airlock door in case of quarantine. Only a handful of chrome and plastic chairs scattered around the compact space, leaving Luis to guess Bitanthrans didn't get sick very often.

A man dressed in a bright blue medical uniform glanced at them from behind the window, then moved to the side. A second later, he opened the airlock door, a huge grin on his dark brown face.

"Good to see you again, Tegwin!" He caught her up in a quick hug. "And you must be Dr. Ahmad. I'm Ben Essena, the head nurse." His broad hand swallowed Luis's, but Ben's grip was easy. "We have everything ready if you are. Need something to drink, anything to eat?"

Luis laughed before he could stop himself. He remembered that from his grandparents as well. The immediate effort to feed anyone who came with their reach.

"Good to meet you, Ben. Call me Luis, please. Nothing to eat, thank you. Myrtle and Willis stuffed us silly. Maybe water for everyone?"

"I'll send some right back." Ben waved his wrist, where the same silver comm-bracelet Tegwin wore caught the light, then held the door open. "This way and we'll get you started."

Luis made a mental note to talk to Ben privately as soon as he could. In a small town hospital, the doctors were wonderful to get to know. But making a friend of the nurses would get him everything he *needed* to know.

Ben probably knew more about the people in this town than Myrtle and Willis. And he'd know who Luis should talk to in town and every tiny settlement tucked into the mountains, and make the introductions to boot.

"Glad to have someone using these suites," Ben said as they followed him down a hallway painted and tiled in cool green. Numbered examination rooms broke up the monotony. "They're usually for new mothers."

The nurse's smile disappeared, and he glanced back at the Becalmed pair.

"Please do not worry." Helen's voice was quiet but clear. "We understand the trouble with new babies. We cannot be offended."

"So the birthrate is dropping?" Luis said, determined to keep Ben talking. And to test how detached the Becalmed truly were.

"Has been for years. People say they're afraid."

"If the birthrate falls too far," Tegwin said, "the colony will collapse on its own."

## Chapter 6

Luis did keep his thoughts to himself despite Helen's reassurance. If TransGalactic let that happen, bringing in short-term workers they paid enough to tolerate long stretches in isolation, part of their problem might solve itself. Assuming Bitanthrans allowed themselves to die out and be replaced.

Ben stopped beside the first of several dark wooden doors, with letters instead of numbers. A, B, C, and so on continued around the corner.

"I do worry about that to tell you the truth." Another wave of the wrist to open the door. "This is one of the suites, just like the rest. Plenty of food in stock, though anyone in town would be delighted to have an off-world guest and talk your ears off. All your things are here already. Yours too, Helen and Willis."

Luis saw his drift of black bags and cases along a cheerful yellow wall. The living space he could see was as modern as the rest of the facility, with a wall mounted entertainment and comm terminal, a compact automated kitchen pod, and a row of windows overlooking a huge garden area that would have been his grandmother's pride. No wonder Bitanthrans ate so well.

"This will open your suite for now." Ben said. Luis took the bright blue identi-badge the nurse held out, then pinned the tiny square to his jacket. "You'll have to have one of us let you into the building, though. Will Dr. Ahmad get a wrist-comm, Tegwin?"

"We can do that if you like, Luis." She peeked into her own suite across the hall, then closed the door. Helen and Willis seemed to already know where they'd be staying. "It would only take a few hours. Might make things easier with such a long assignment."

Ben backtracked up the hall to a solid metal white door.

"This is the biggest procedure room we have here. Big enough for four beds and all the monitoring equipment you could ever need. Your headgear arrived not long before you did, Dr. Ahmad."

Luis followed the nurse into a room utterly at odds with the slow-paced, rustic town he knew was outside. The walls and ceiling looked like dimpled cream-colored fabric, perfectly designed to dampen any noise. What Ben called beds were as far away from flat, traditional mattresses, or the bunks even on a ship as fine as the *Bountyfield.*

Thick, tan padding lined a reclining surface that offered adjustments for not only the back, but also for all four limbs and the head. He suspected leaning back into that padding would feel like floating on warm air.

Whatever their motivation, TransGalactic spared no expense in looking after the health of people mining and supporting Bitan.

Sleek, oval pods that adjusted to any height stood beside each bed. Luis would need those for monitoring heartbeat and respiration. His primary equipment, four shiny black cases shaped like human skulls, waited on a table in the middle of the room.

Luis pressed his fingertips into the top of one, much like his sphere reader, then lifted the thin lid. The psych-hypnosis nets were as fine and intricate as black lace, with glittering red sensor nodes instead of hand-tied knots. His subjects always said they couldn't feel the nets at all.

Luis turned back to the group, then blinked. Helen and Willis were each stretched out on an exam table, hands folded over their bellies. Both stared up at the ceiling, faces calm and blank.

"I usually explain things a little more, answer questions," he said. "Before we get started."

Helen turned her eyes toward him without moving her head.

"We have no questions, Dr. Ahmad. You can ask us any questions you want to."

"Please, everyone, call me Luis." He shrugged and shook his head. "If everyone else is ready, we can get started with the initial calibration and setup."

As Luis fitted the nets onto Helen and Willis, thankful for their short hair, he wondered if sedation would be necessary at all with the Becalmed.

"Okay, we're ready to begin," he said. "This might be a little boring, but be patient with me, and with the systems. Once we have your brains mapped, we'll…we'll get to more interesting questions."

Luis shook his head, reminding himself he might have to adjust his usual testing speech. He normally joked about not being afraid of a scan finding nothing in the brain at all, getting down to the fun part and rearranging thoughts and memories, silly things to put the subjects at ease.

Helen and Drew probably wouldn't have a problem with

what he said. But joking about the problem he was here to diagnose felt more than a little insensitive to him.

"We're ready, Luis," Drew said.

"You won't feel anything, so just relax." Luis tapped the interface on the skull-shaped control units, linking them to the oval bedside pods. "If you would, please count silently starting with one. However fast or slow you want, but for this part, stay with whole numbers. One, two, three. I'm going to activate a white noise field so you can concentrate. We'll switch it up in a little while."

He started the sound generator embedded in the sensor nets. He heard only a faint whisper of static, but anyone wearing the net would hear nothing else in the room.

Luis crossed his arms and waited for data, watching Helen and Drew's mouths move as they counted. Tegwin stood beside him, her head tilted.

"It's mapping the physical brain?"

"That's the first step. It goes from the outside in, mapping deeper and more complex structures as it goes. There's the first set."

The displays showed a faint blue outline of a human brain, wrinkly with two matched halves. Red dots filled in slowly, marking the curves and folds under the surface.

"We'll switch to more complex numbers, counting by twos and threes. Then the alphabet, and words. What I'm worried about is the next phase."

"Emotional mapping," Tegwin said, glancing at Helen and Drew. "That's getting into memories, right?"

"Exactly. They should do fine with earliest memories, when they started school, when they finished school. Then things like waking up this morning, when they met me, when they put the nets on. But will they even understand when I ask about a happiest moment, times when they were afraid or sad?"

"A whole lot of people are interested in the answer to that."

The emotional mapping questions, and the resulting data, were less dramatic and far less informative than Luis expected. Helen and Drew simply looked straight up at the ceiling when he asked, like they did with all the other questions. But neither of them responded to any questions about strong feelings.

"Okay, that's all we need right now," Luis said. He glanced at Tegwin, raising his eyebrows and shaking his head. "You two can take a break, go out and walk around for a bit. I know it's hard to be still for that long. Thank you."

The two of them sat up, waiting for Luis to remove the nets. Both ran their fingers through their short hair, but they didn't laugh or comment on the experience like most subjects did.

"Thank you, Luis. When should we be back here?"

"What is it here, sweeps instead of hours? We've been here two sweeps. Be back in one?"

Both Helen and Drew nodded, then left without another word.

Luis moved his rolling chair beside the table holding the net's sensor units and sat with a gusty sigh.

"Well, that tells us exactly nothing."

"How so?" Tegwin said.

She leaned over his shoulder, watching the units light up with a replay of the tests. The red dots aligned themselves inside the translucent skulls, recreating Helen and Drew's brains. The marks were unnaturally regular and evenly spaced.

"This is the same thing you'd see in a classroom or textbook. Not one for alternate development or various thinking styles, either. This is the standard, off the rack, learning-the-basics human brain pattern. Helen and Drew show no deviation whatsoever."

"You mean nothing abnormal?"

"I mean nothing at all. Not even normal deviations that we all have. Someone could have assembled their brains out of a beginner textbook. Even though they didn't answer the questions, the emotional responses worked within their brains. But those were identical to each other. That's not possible in humans. Not that I've ever seen."

Tegwin sat beside him, rubbing her face.

"So all we've learned is we're not going to find the problem in their brains."

"Right. Though I'd say this kind of utterly standard development is a problem in itself. If I got these results on any other subject, I'd suspect the units were malfunctioning."

"But these are brand new and calibrated." Tegwin pulled out her own spherical display device, glancing at the surface. "Nine sweeps ago. I did it myself."

Luis shrugged. "I'll run diagnostics again, but I promise they'll come up functioning perfectly. I want to test typical subjects to make sure, of course. Something else is going on here."

"I may not have much authority as your planetary liaison," Tegwin said. She stood, leaning back with her hands on her hips. "But I'm going to use it. Take your own advice, Luis. Start the diagnostics, but get out of here for a little while. Walk around and get some fresh air. Think about something else. That's what I'm going to do."

# Chapter 7

As soon as Luis stepped out into the corridor, he knew he was going to ignore part of what Tegwin said. He spotted Ben in the nurses' office, chatting with one of the doctors on duty. Luis was willing to bet the healthy population allowed for a few unscheduled breaks for medical personnel.

Ben smiled when he caught sight of Luis.

"Everything going well back there?"

"Good so far, Ben. Just finished up the initial mapping and calibration. Listen, if you have a few minutes, I'd love to speak to you."

"You bet. When we actually do have an emergency around here, it can be a bad one. But most of the time, we're pretty laid back. Walk with me?"

"Show me your town."

A few minutes of walking through the cool, sunny afternoon with Ben's easy narration revived Luis more than he expected. Several general stores. Banking and travel planning. Charming but modern schools for children. Even a small college to start adults on the paths to careers other than mining.

Luis found nothing out of the ordinary among the wooden and stone buildings, the neat and well-maintained businesses and streets. But the fresh air and conversation stirred up enough questions that he wasn't sure where to start.

When they settled into a loop around a path that circled downtown, lined with flowerbeds and stone gardens, Ben made it a lot easier.

"I imagine you have more serious things to ask me about than the town gossip," he said with a smile. "Go right ahead. That's what I'm here for."

"TransGalactic warned you about me?"

"I wouldn't say warned. They mentioned that you'd want someone to talk to. Someone who knows more about the people who live here than they do themselves."

"That I want. Promise you'll tell me if I'm asking things you'd rather not answer?"

Ben brushed his fingertips through a chest-high bush covered with tiny burgundy flowers. The stirred up aroma smelled like fresh apples to Luis.

"I've been watching this place try to die out for years now. No matter what any of us do, the trouble is only getting worse. As far as I'm concerned, nothing is off limits."

Luis tried to organize his thoughts for several steps before he gave up.

"I've had the briefings, read the reports. I'll test Myrtle and Willis when we get back, but I don't think I'll find anything out of the ordinary with them, either. What do you think I need to know, Ben?"

"Find anything with Helen and Drew? Anything unusual?"

Luis shook his head. "Probably not the way you mean. The only thing their brains are missing is any kind of deviation. They test out like someone picked up standard human brains off a shelf and installed them. Even the emotional centers are normal. And identical to each other."

"Wish I could say I was surprised. We haven't been able to do anything like your psych-hypnosis or that kind of deep brain scan. But the Becalmed always act like every other kid when they're born. By the time they start school, though, around five years old, they change."

"No trauma, no difference in their nutrition or experiences?"

"Not a thing. The hardest part has been watching siblings grow up and grow apart. We had several sets of twins over the years, one typical, one Becalmed. The last three sets of twins born are both Becalmed."

Luis watched a group of kids running around outside the primary school. His heart sank at his quick count. About half were laughing and squealing, playing like any kids he'd ever seen.

The other half walked around the edges of the playground, nearly in lockstep. Eerily silent. Their faces weren't sad or angry. They were simply as calm and blank as Helen and Drew.

"How about the rest of the population?" Luis said.

"You mean mentally, emotionally? They're fairly average humans, I'd say. I was off-world for a few years doing my medical training, but I've lived here the rest of my life. The only thing I noticed is how much everyone who's born here loves Bitanthra."

"You too?"

"Absolutely. I hated being away from here, every second of it. Now, I know everyone gets homesick. This is different from what I can tell. Being away, even on the orbital med base to help out with childbirth, feels like a part of me is missing. And that missing part hurts, like a broken bone or something. We have to take shifts up there because none of us can stand it for long."

A warm, tingly space in Luis's chest woke up. That tingle was usually his first hint of how he would find a solution, or at least part of it. He knew better than to worry about that just yet. His idea seed needed time and space to grow.

"How are people reacting? Besides the Becalmed?"

This time Ben took several steps before answering. Luis concentrated on their footsteps crunching through black gravel, not wanting to interrupt or rush.

"I generally see folks once a year for a physical, and that's it. We can schedule those like clockwork, hardly any deviation at all, except for accidents at the mines or somewhere else. Lately, though, people have been coming in at odd times. Mostly women, but a few men."

He walked quietly again, leaving Luis hoping he didn't know the reason for the strange visits. His chest told him he did.

"They're coming in for birth control," Ben said. "Even the ones who don't have any kids. We don't have any problem with that here, not at all. But the whole planet has a problem when more than half the adult population doesn't want children. Not because of some personal reason or to concentrate on their work, or because they have enough. We always had that. People are coming in now because they're too afraid to try."

"How do they feel about the Becalmed, Ben? How do you feel?"

"You met Helen and Drew. They're sweet as they can be, never would hurt anything or anyone. Most people seem to know this isn't contagious, or at least we don't think it is. But it's not just the Becalmed who are happier about their separate community."

Luis tried to find something to say, some way to reassure Ben. But the truth was he had nothing but more questions, and more worries than he had when they'd started walking.

"I'll do everything I can to figure this out, Ben. I give you my word."

# Chapter 8

By the time Luis and Ben got back to the medical facility, everybody was waiting for them in the lobby. Luis noticed how Helen and Drew sat quietly off to the side, while Tegwin chatted with Myrtle and Willis.

Humans always sorted themselves into groups, just like almost any living thing. That in itself wasn't a problem. But the lack of basic understanding between these two groups was starting to frighten him after only a few hours.

The separation continued as he got Myrtle and Willis set up for their own calibration and testing. Helen and Drew volunteered to go wait in their rooms instead of observing, and no one besides Luis seemed disturbed by that. The only thing he could think of was to agree and move on.

A couple of sweeps later, with the leaders of the typical Bitanthrans departed for the evening and Helen and Drew still in their rooms, Luis and Tegwin watched the calibration results pop up in the second set of skulls.

"See the difference?" Luis said. He'd left Helen and Drew's sensors active on the other side of the table for comparison.

"They're all over the place." Tegwin walked around the table, leaning down to peer through the two sets of results. "I don't think one point matches between Myrtle and Willis."

"Nope, and they wouldn't between me and you. They're hitting in the typical regions of the brain, sure, but not nearly so regular."

She crossed her arms, looking at Luis.

"They acted different during the testing, too. They weren't just following instructions, were they? They were living those memories. I saw it on their faces, in their bodies. The monitors picked it up in their vital signs, too."

"Especially the bad ones." Luis waited for the soft chime of a completed brain map before pulling one of the oval display pods over to the table. "That's exactly what I think Helen and Drew were doing. Following what I said with no emotional responses, at least not that they were aware of. Their brains reacted accordingly."

He tapped the display to zoom in on the right side of Myrtle's brain, toward the front. The red dots increased in both size and frequency.

"Remember your theory about the typical Bitanthran being a bit more emotional than usual? That's what we see in Myrtle, in response to the bad and good memories." He pulled up Willis's brain. The dots were in different places, but also large and close together. "Same with Willis. This doesn't look like any kind of disorder, but it is on the high end of normal."

Tegwin leaned down again, examining the right sides of each of the translucent skulls.

"But in Helen and Drew, everything is tiny, spaced out. Almost like a grid."

"Right," Luis said. "Regular enough to read as unnatural."

Tegwin walked around the exam room, seeming to peer

at every display and piece of equipment. Luis would have bet his credit bonus for this mission she wasn't seeing a single bit of it.

He wished he had one of the sensory nets set on her right now. He'd watched the human mind make connections and leaps countless times in demonstrations and tests, but he never tired of seeing that magic.

"This isn't making sense, Luis." Tegwin still had her back turned, still walking. "Helen and Drew's results may be too normal, but they *are* happening."

"Right."

"And you just said Helen and Drew could be having emotional responses that they're not aware of."

"I did. I'd love to have a sensor net on them when they're asleep. See if they're dreaming and not remembering it, too. Have you seen reports of the scans they can do here or on the orbital med base?"

She turned to face him, one eyebrow raised.

"They show as normal. Nowhere as accurate as what you just did, not as detailed. But still, normal. You think they've got some kind of block."

"With what we've seen so far," he said, "nothing else makes sense. I can't imagine people here are hiding any kind of trauma, and I'm seeing no signs of disease. I can't explain it yet, but yeah. I think there's a block."

"You've dealt with blocks in deep psych-hypnosis before, right?"

Now Luis stood, walking back to the exam beds. He touched the head rest on one, tapping his fingers on the soft surface.

"Many times. But they were usually the result of an injury or emotional trauma. Sometimes a disease or disorder. I'm afraid we'll rule all of that out with our first session tomorrow. Helen and Drew appear to be perfectly healthy. If anything, their brains are *too* healthy. I have no idea what we're dealing with here, Tegwin."

He was surprised to see her smile.

"And I was worried about this being just another boring assignment in the middle of nowhere."

## Chapter 9

A RESTLESS NIGHT, unlike Luis usually had first night planetside, and a fruitless first morning of psych-hypnosis did nothing to improve his gloomy mood. Just as before, Helen and Drew answered every question, followed every last bit of instruction.

And just as before, even under the deep psych field, they showed no conscious emotional response to any prompt.

The emotional centers of the brain throughout the limbic system continued to react, laying down more perfect and regular dots on their sensor displays. But even with the diagnostic bed's sensory arrays active, Luis detected no physical response. Their placid expressions and voices matched their unchanging heart rate and respiration, body temperature and perspiration.

If he didn't know he was working with flesh and blood humans, Luis would have sworn he was examining the most lifelike simulations ever created.

The only event that broke up the growing frustration, and his hovering sense of hopelessness, was Tegwin returning from her midday break with a fitting bracelet. She slipped what felt like a smooth, silver chain around his left wrist.

"I'm getting my own tiny piece of Bitan?"

"So tiny." The cool metal shifted and formed itself, tickling the hair for a few seconds, before she clicked it open. "You know Earth sand? Or maybe a grain of salt?"

"Hardly worth a fortune, huh?"

"Not exactly. Even the highest level officers of Trans-Galactic get the same thing. Sadly, since you're technically a contractor on Bitanthra, they'll want this back before you leave."

Luis rolled his eyes and rubbed his wrist. He welcomed Tegwin's touch behind his own, enjoying the warm sensations her fingers stirred up a long way down.

"Think I'll get to touch any Bitan? That I can actually see, I mean?"

Tegwin slipped the silver bracelet into a flat black box.

"We should be able to head up into the mountains at some point. I doubt we can go into the deep mining chambers, but there's always plenty at the surface, where they process the ore."

"That would be something different," Luis said. He activated the second set of sensors, getting ready for the first round of deep psych for Myrtle and Willis. "Unlike what we're getting in here."

"You can't be getting discouraged already. How many days do you usually test each subject before you start working on their problems? Just the one?"

Luis glanced over his shoulder, making sure she was smiling.

"Usually at least a week. Often a lot longer on more complex problems. But I normally see something in the first few tests, you know? Some idea of where to head next."

"You're asking the same questions with Myrtle and

Willis?" Tegwin said. She flipped through her notes on her holo-reader.

"That's right, a general hypnosis session. Make sure the psych field is working, gather responses to compare to the Becalmed. Something you think I should be watching for?"

She shook her head, but she was frowning.

"Not really." She jumped at a knock on the exam room door. "That's Myrtle and Willis. I don't know, just remember those high emotional responses. Okay?"

She opened the door before Luis could respond.

"Come on in, he's ready for you."

The contrast from the tranquility of Helen and Drew was obvious from the second Myrtle and Willis walked in. They didn't look angry, exactly, but Luis could see from their hard expressions and stiff gaits that they were nervous. And not happy about feeling that way.

"There's nothing to worry about," he said. "This won't be all that different from the testing and calibration yesterday."

Myrtle pressed her lips together until they were a thin line.

"This is the part where you hypnotize us, right?"

She crossed the room and sat on one of the exam beds, but her entire body remained tense.

"We generate a field from the brain map we made yesterday." Luis touched the skull unit with Myrtle's data, and it glowed with dots, lines, and folds. "This won't make you act strangely or let me control your mind. We'll just be able to ask questions you may not usually be able to answer."

Willis sat on his own bed, looking nearly as anxious as Myrtle.

"They explained all of this to us," he said. "The people from TransG. Before we said we would help, and we still want to help. It's just different walking in here knowing you're going to poke around in our brains."

"You use this for criminals?" Myrtle said. "To make them confess?"

"We can't do that, no." Luis kept the dubious origins of the technology to himself, just like most people in his line of work did. Along with the differing laws for wartime or galactic-level crimes. "Forced confession is illegal. People who work with criminals use deep psych when the accused ask for it. To verify the things they're saying, since no one can lie under the field. We don't force them to do anything. The only similarity here is we record your words along with your data, but like we discussed before, that doesn't leave this room without your permission."

"Do you do that sometimes, though?" Willis said. "With criminals?"

"No, not even during my training. I've always worked with people who have some kind of problem with their brains. Injuries, certain diseases. Sometimes an emotional trauma they need help with."

Myrtle and Willis locked gazes. Luis knew he'd led them right to the questions they really wanted to ask. Myrtle looked into his eyes.

"You think that's what happens to them? Some kind of trauma? Or a disease?"

Luis sat on the rolling chair he'd pulled beside the beds while he was working with Helen and Drew.

"We don't know what's going on, but I don't think it's trauma. I see no signs of disease. With the way it only affects some people in a family, I don't believe this is contagious at all. Mind if I ask you a question?"

Both Bitanthrans shook their heads.

"What do you think is going on? What do people who live here, who've been watching this happen for years, think?"

Willis drew in a slow breath, and Luis saw tears standing in his eyes.

"Some of us are afraid it's poison, something to do with Bitan. It seems to be getting worse over time. Like we've been exposed too much, and we're passing it along to our children."

"Well, I can't rule anything out yet since we just got started. But your medical center here has tested for everything we know of, and off-world facilities have too. Nothing seems out of line with your bodies. Nothing seems to accumulate or get depleted over time."

"Except our kids' feelings," Myrtle said. She didn't look sad like Willis. She looked furious. "That's depleting, more and more every year."

"I can only imagine how hard that's been for all of you," Luis said. "I know you're scared and upset. I'm going to do everything I can to help. I promise I won't hurt you along the way. Okay?"

Myrtle stared into his eyes, and Luis knew any planetary system court's specialized deep psych equipment wouldn't see him any more clearly than she did.

"Okay. We'll do whatever we can to help you do that."

She lay back on the bed, letting it adjust her into the best position for testing. Willis nodded once at Luis, then he did the same.

He and Tegwin fitted the sensor nets, then Luis held his hands over the skull units.

"Starting the field in three...two...one."

He touched the plastic temples with his fingertip and thumb, then tapped the top of the skulls. Myrtle and Willis didn't react, but the maps in front of Luis glowed green. The display of brain waves on the oval viewing pods gradually changed from a chaotic bunch of peaks and valleys to slow rises and falls.

"We're ready to begin," Luis said, sitting down beside the beds again.

He worked through the typical list of baseline questions, letting the field adjust and fine tune itself. Name, occupation, age. Last things they ate or drank, who they talked to on the way to the facility. Myrtle and Willis responded much the same ways Helen and Drew did, as Luis expected.

"Now, Willis, I'm going to ask you a different kind of question. One you answered for me earlier. I'm not trying to trick you. This just lets us get an idea if the field is adjusted to your brains. What do you think is causing the trouble with the Becalmed?"

Willis answered the same way he had before, almost word for word. His emotional responses jumped up, too, all over the right side of his brain. Fear and sadness ticked outside of normal, not quite into disordered levels. Tears escaped his closed eyes, running down his cheeks.

"Thank you, Willis. Myrtle, I didn't ask you this before, but I want to know what you think is going on with the Becalmed."

"Poison, like Willis says." Myrtle's readings lit up bright around the amygdala. Fear, again, and especially high levels of anger. "Not from here, though. Not from the Bitan we bring up out of the ground. Somewhere else. Far away from here."

Luis looked at Tegwin, eyebrows raised. She shrugged and shook her head.

"Can you tell me more about that, Myrtle? Why you'd say that?"

"You asked me what I thought. I told you. That's all."

Her levels calmed when Luis moved on to emotional mapping, never getting to the same peak of intensity. Not with questions designed to elicit fear, sadness, even anger.

She and Willis both responded within typical human emotional range, all across the spectrum. Neither reached the high peaks brought on by the question about the Becalmed.

## Chapter 10

Tegwin's grin when Luis walked into the exam room the next day was too infectious to resist, even after he'd slept less than the night before.

"You're not under house arrest anymore," she said, holding out a small black bag. "You won't have to track me or Ben down to get in or out of this place, either. Or into another apartment if you're interested."

Inside was a thin silver bracelet, less than half the width of Luis's pinkie finger. It was open, hinged in the middle underneath the blue and gold TransGalactic logo. When Luis closed it around his wrist, it fit perfectly against every contour of his flesh and bone.

"I'm very interested in other apartments," he said, returning her smile. "At least one other one. How do I get it back off?"

"You don't," Tegwin said. "Not until you're ready to leave. I've been wearing mine for almost twenty years now. Well, a lot longer than that if you count my hyper-sleep time, but I try not to. If it needs adjustments, let me know. But it should fit close enough that you won't notice it."

Luis made a fist and flexed his wrist in a circle, watching the wrist-comm flash and shift.

"I already can't really feel it. What all will this do for me?"

"Mainly opening the doors in and out of here. There aren't any other secured facilities to speak of in this part of Bitanthra. If you go down to the resorts, this won't get you in to the vaults in the gaming areas or anything like that. Otherwise, you should be set."

She turned to activate the deep psych equipment, then turned back.

"It's a tracker, too. They all are, not just yours. Some people don't like that, I know, but it's more in case someone has an accident than anything else. Just thought you should know."

"Thanks for the warning," Luis said. "I'm not that exciting to track. I might get out and see the town tonight though, instead of huddling in my rooms."

"You told me you wanted to be alone for a couple of days! I would have invited you…" Tegwin stopped, catching sight of his expression. "Well done, you got me. You're still welcome to join me if you want."

The flirty mood evaporated as Luis glanced over his notes from the past couple of days, along with his notes from a nearly sleepless night. If he kept getting the same results, or lack of results, he was going to have to let his superiors know he was out of ideas.

That was a conversation he hadn't had since his fledgling days, when none of them truly understood how the psych fields worked. Luis and everyone else in the field had to read questions from a list back then. He didn't want to have that conversation now after decades of experience, but he was running out of ideas.

Luis knew something had changed as soon as he activated the deep psych field for Helen.

The red dots in the emotional centers, all around the amygdala, glowed more brightly than before. He was sure they were lighting up in different areas, too. Not just the textbook locations from before.

"How you feeling today, Helen?" he said.

"I am fine," she said. The strained tone in her voice made Tegwin and even Drew look up. "No, that's not the truth. I felt normal until I got here. Until you put the sensor net on my head."

"And now?" Luis stood beside her, checking the placement of the glittering red sensory nodes against her short hair. "What's different?"

She shook her head, but not hard enough to dislodge the black netting.

"My shoulders hurt. My jaws." She opened and closed her fists, then rubbed her palms against her thighs. People usually didn't move once they were under the field. "Everything feels too tight."

"Your voice sounds too tight," Drew said. His expression remained calm, but he watched Helen closely. "Are you ill?"

"That's not your business!"

As soon as she said it, Helen's eyes opened wide. She covered her mouth with one hand.

"Luis," Tegwin said. "The readings."

Luis turned the oval readout toward him. Instead of regular waves, not much different than a brain under the deep psych field, Helen's emotional lines were jagged and sharp. Almost as sharp as Myrtle's had been.

"Same thing on the other sensor," Luis said, glancing that way. "More points showing up as we speak."

"Something is wrong with me," Helen said, her voice

trembling now. "My throat is hot and swelling up. My face, too. I have a fever."

"I don't think it's a fever," Luis said. "Nothing is wrong. But something is different. Did you do anything unusual last night or this morning? Outside of what you normally do?"

She shook her head again, this time causing the net to shift to the side. Luis adjusted it, watching the readings jump again.

"Nothing different. All I've done different is coming in here," she said, her voice rising. "Letting you look at my brain. Is this all because of your deep psych?"

Luis blinked, opening, then closing his mouth.

"I don't think…I don't know. We've never done this kind of testing on the Becalmed before. Not on anyone on Bitanthra, actually. The testing itself should be neutral, but something is changing. That could be it. Are you willing to continue?"

She stared at him, chin quivering.

"Is this going to go away? When the tests stop?"

"Do you want it to, Helen?" Tegwin said, standing on the other side of the bed. Luis saw several more bright red points appear inside the translucent skull.

"I don't like whatever is happening to me. I said I would help you, though, find out what's happening with the babies. I didn't say I wanted you to change me."

"We don't have to keep going," Luis said. He wanted to jump in and figure this out, badly, and right now. But he couldn't stand the frightened look in eyes and a face so clearly unused to such things. "All of this is voluntary, remember? Every bit of it is up to you."

Helen turned toward Drew, and Luis followed her gaze. The Becalmed man still seemed unfazed, not caught up in whatever was affecting Helen.

Drew didn't have his sensor net on yet, either.

"You can keep going," Helen said, drawing Luis's attention back. "As long as you promise me you'll try to fix this. Whatever is wrong with me."

"I don't know if I can, Helen. I can't promise that."

"But you'll try to, right? I want to help, but you have to promise you'll try."

Tears rolled down her cheeks, and she drew back, as if she could escape them. Luis felt his own eyes welling up.

"I will try, Helen. I promise."

"Go ahead, then. I'll do my best."

"We'll try just with Helen if that's okay with you, Drew." Luis waited for the Becalmed man to nod. "Then we'll focus on you."

Luis turned back to activate the deep psych field, hoping he hadn't made a promise to Helen that he couldn't keep.

"Activating field in three…two…one. Still doing okay, Helen?"

"I still don't feel good, but you go ahead."

"Now that you're under, let me ask you if you know what's changed today. What's different?"

Helen's smooth face wrinkled around her eyes and nose, the first time she'd reacted that way to anything.

"My belly is all stirred up and my back and neck hurt, and I feel like hot water is sloshing around in my chest. My throat, too. If this is what everyone else lives with, you can keep it. I'd rather stay Becalmed."

"I hope we can do that for you," Luis said. "Do you feel like some part of your mind is open now? Something you couldn't get to yesterday?"

"Only the part that's all agitated and shaky, not like part of me at all. Something outside of me, so far I can't reach it. But it can reach me."

Luis caught Tegwin's gaze. So close to what Myrtle said

about the Becalmed and the poison. That it all came from far away.

"I won't keep you under too long today, Helen. I'll ask you a few more questions, then I'll let you relax. We'll talk to Drew."

Drew and his scans were nearly the same as Helen's. He got more anxious as soon as Luis slipped his sensor net into place, and the questions only made it worse. Luis decided to cut their sessions short rather than risk causing them too much upset.

He'd never worked with or even heard of humans with no emotional responses. He'd certainly never worked with humans who suddenly gained that ability as adults, with no preparation or warning.

Luis did not want to wade too deeply into that territory without a whole lot more preparation, for himself and the Becalmed. Especially with two people who had no interest in the changes being permanent.

"Tegwin, can you help me with his net for a second? We're just about finished."

When she leaned in, the number of red marks in Drew's sensor jumped up again. Luis froze, his hand on one side of the man's head, Tegwin's on the other.

"Wait," he said, not wanting to scare the Becalmed any more than they already were. "Tegwin, reach toward me. Toward my hand."

This time, the readings on the viewscreen spiked. Drew groaned, and sweat broke out on his face. Luis saw muscles tense up all over his body.

"Are you in pain, Drew?" Tegwin said. "Does some part of your body hurt?"

"Nothing hurts. Not like that. Not my arms or my legs. My chest hurts, my stomach. My head feels like it's going to fly apart!"

Luis and Tegwin both stepped back, eyes wide. Luis held his hands over the plastic skull emanating the deep psych field for Drew.

"Okay, Drew, I'm going to stop the field now. You'll feel better in just a second. Ending field in three…two…one."

As soon as Luis touched the sensor temples, Drew's drawn up body relaxed. He opened reddened, watering eyes and sighed.

"Same thing happened to me as Helen," he said, looking from Tegwin to Luis. "Same exact thing. What are you doing to us?"

The warm tingle in Luis's chest, his hint that he was onto something, flared up into a raging fire. He knew his face was as flushed as Drew's was, and he smelled his own sweat. He didn't feel like he could possibly reassure anyone at the moment, but he had to try.

"I'm sorry this happened," he said, grabbing Drew's arm to help him sit up. "What I told Helen is the truth. We've never worked with the Becalmed before. You're helping chart new territory here, and we appreciate it more than I can say."

Drew blotted his face with his shirt sleeve, staring at the damp spots. Luis saw faint lines on Drew's smooth flesh when he turned back.

"That's not what I thought I'd be doing when I woke up this morning. You people walk around feeling like this all the time? Is that what it is?"

"Not all the time, thank goodness," Tegwin said. She kept glancing at Luis, her face pale. "But that might be what's happening. If you've never had emotional responses before, it would probably be quite uncomfortable."

Helen hadn't moved or said a word. She sat watching on her own exam bed, and the tight set of her eyes and mouth made Luis think she wasn't quite back to her Becalmed self.

"Are you feeling better, Helen?" he said. "Now that you're out of the field?"

She stared at him for a few seconds, her eyes stony and cold. Luis was amazed how such a small difference changed her whole face.

"I feel better, sure. I don't like how upset Drew was just now. Has this whole thing been about trying to trick us? Fix us? Make us more like you?"

Luis closed his eyes, shaking his head. His internal fire died down, but it didn't quite go out.

"No, not at all. I've helped people work better with their emotions, but only if they wanted me to. I didn't expect this to happen."

She nodded, her eyes still cold.

"Want to call it off for today?" Luis said. "Let us do a little research, see if we can figure this out? Maybe once you two are away from here for a while, back to your normal routine, you'll feel more like yourselves."

"I hope so," Helen said. She stood and held out her hand to Drew. "I sure do hope so. We'll be back in the morning."

Drew took her hand and stood beside her, and they walked toward the door together.

Right before he stepped out, Drew turned back to Luis and smiled.

# Chapter 11

Tegwin closed the door behind the Becalmed couple, then leaned against it. She took a deep breath before she spoke.

"What just happened, Luis? What did we do to them?"

Luis squeezed his temples, trying to slow his spinning thoughts.

"I don't think we did anything. But something changed. I have to get out of here. Walk with me?"

Neither spoke until they got to the path around downtown. The same one where Luis had walked with Ben in what felt like a different lifetime. The sky was the same deep blue where the heavy cloud cover broke, the trees and grass the same rich shades of green.

The same bunches of school kids sorted themselves into groups on the playground, one half laughing and playing. Luis couldn't drag his gaze away from the group walking in silent circles around the fence.

"Are we changing them, Luis? Is deep psych some kind of a cure?"

"I don't think it's the psych field." He held up his wrist,

turning the bracelet so it caught the scattered sunlight. "I think it's this. And I don't believe Helen would call it a cure at all."

"Bitan? They've been around that their whole lives. Is there any in your sensory nets, or the field generator?"

"Not even a bit of dust. That's one of the few tech devices I know of that uses no Bitan at all. Put those two together, though, and we may have an entirely different field. Maybe a much stronger one. People don't usually move under deep psych, but they both did."

They walked in silence for several minutes. Luis brushed his fingers through the chest-high bush like Ben had, holding his hand up to breathe in the fresh apple scent. Forcing himself into physical reality, trying to slow his thoughts enough to catch them.

He lowered his hand, accidently touching Tegwin's. She brought him all the way out of his mind and into his body when she twined her warm fingers through his.

"What do we do now?" she said. "I'm not so sure Helen or Drew will be willing to work with us anymore after today. Do we try to find people willing to try it, knowing what might happen?"

"I think Drew will be back. Did you see his eyes when he left? You're probably right about Helen, but Drew liked what he felt. That doesn't mean we can just experiment on them, though."

"He gave consent, didn't he? We just explain how things have changed. I think he understands that better than we do, anyway. Then we could try. This could help all those kids, Luis. This could keep Bitanthra from collapsing, which it *will* in less than fifty years."

Luis looked down at his bracelet, where the tiny grain of Bitan was. He still hadn't seen any.

"Tegwin, you mentioned getting up to the mines,

getting a look at Bitan and how they extract it. If that's what made the difference, the tiny bit in this bracelet, more deep psych alone may not be the answer even if Drew does agree. Is there someone on the surface who can authorize us getting more of it? Getting some larger pieces for the exam room?"

"See if it will amplify the effect, whatever it is." She pursed her lips. "Probably not anyone on the surface, since they're still meeting up on the *Bountyfield*. Almost everyone with authority on Bitanthra is there. A whole lot of people with TransGalactic authority, too."

"I probably shouldn't say this to my planetary liaison, but can we work with the Bitanthrans instead of TransG?"

She stopped, turning to face him.

"Why? What do you think they'll object to?"

Luis shrugged, holding up his free hand.

"I don't know, maybe nothing. Probably nothing. But this does concern everyone on this planet more than anyone else. It's their children, their way of life threatened."

"The whole galaxy is concerned with Bitan production, Luis. That's what this whole thing is about. Without it-"

"I know, I understand. That is why I'm here. You know how slow a big corporation can be. They control Bitan, but they send people through years of hypersleep for a meeting! We might be days or weeks waiting for approval. Maybe months. We might not get approval at all. I want to try to help these people. Figure this out. Why would TransGalactic care *how* if we solve their problem?"

Tegwin grabbed his other hand, squeezing her eyes closed for a moment before she stared into his.

"Okay, listen," she said. "Ben comes from a mining family, one of the first to settle on the planet. His father is on the management level that goes to these big meetings up on the *Bountyfield*, but he always stays to coordinate from here. I think he's actually in charge of planetary operations right now."

"No one knows what's going on better than Ben," Luis said. "He sees these families all the time, all year long."

"Let's go talk to him, then. See what he thinks. I can't promise any of this will work, but I'm willing to try."

# Chapter 12

THEY FOUND Ben back at the medical facility, sitting in the lobby with a young woman. She didn't look much out of her teen years, with skin nearly as dark as Ben's and an upward tilt to her eyes. She leaned forward with her elbows on her knees, sobbing.

Ben glanced up at Luis when he and Tegwin walked in, his own eyes red. He rubbed the woman's back but didn't say anything.

Another nurse opened the office window, waving Luis and Tegwin over.

"Is anything wrong? I saw Helen and Drew leave a while ago."

"We're fine," Tegwin said, keeping her voice low. "We need to speak to Ben whenever he's free. Can you let him know, please?"

The door beside the nurse's window opened, and a woman's voice called the younger woman. She scrubbed at her eyes, hugged Ben, and walked inside.

When the door closed, Ben let out a long, low sigh.

"More and more every day," he said, looking into Luis's eyes. "What can I help you two with?"

"Got a minute to come back to our exam room?" Luis said. "We may be getting closer to figuring this out."

When Luis closed the door, Ben spoke before anyone else could.

"What's going on with Helen and Drew? Neither one of them looked happy when they left. Seeing normal expressions on their faces bothered me more than I thought it would."

"That's what we may need your help with," Luis said. "We used the deep field with them yesterday, no real result. Then today, they both responded. They'd calmed down a lot by the time you saw them."

"You mean they responded emotionally?"

"Not only responded." Tegwin pointed to the still-lit skulls displaying the Becalmed couple's brain maps. "Their brains mapped to new points. Strongly."

Luis held up his wrist. "We think the difference was this. I didn't get it until this morning. When Tegwin stepped close to help me with Drew, he got even more emotional."

Ben sat on one of the exam tables, tilting his head to the side.

"You think Bitan cures them? They've never lived anywhere but here."

"That's what I thought, too," Tegwin said. "Luis told me deep psych has never been used here, and the field doesn't use any Bitan. The two together may work differently. We don't know if it's a cure, but it's doing something."

"They didn't seem hurt in any way?" Ben said. "I've never seen any of the Becalmed as upset as they were, especially Helen."

"I don't think they were hurt," Luis said. "Not physically.

Surprised for certain. Drew wasn't as upset as Helen. I think he'd be willing to try more."

"That young woman out there," Ben said, rubbing the back of his neck. "She just got engaged a few days ago. She was in here begging me to help her, to make sure she doesn't get pregnant. Begging me not to tell her family. Or her fiancé. If we can stop this from getting worse, I'll do whatever I can. Do you need more subjects to work with?"

"Maybe, but not yet." Luis sat on the exam table opposite Ben. "What we really need is more Bitan. Larger pieces of it. I don't think the deep psych field alone is doing this."

"I thought your father might be able to help us," Tegwin said. "We're hoping to see if it works before we involve Trans-Galactic directly. They might make us wait a long, long time before they make a decision."

Ben nodded once, then jumped to his feet.

"They have to spend a couple of years in hypersleep before they make any damn decision. Come on, close up here for the day. I'll take you on a field trip out to the mines. Time to see what makes Bitanthra and this whole galaxy run."

## Chapter 13

Luis regretted his big breakfast before they even got off the ground.

They'd returned to the same transit zone where he and Tegwin arrived, but none of the big, smooth official shuttles waited for them. Ben walked toward a tiny model, with four cramped seats up front and an open, flat cargo bed in the back.

"How far is the mine?" Luis said, his jaws already aching. "Can we get there another way?"

"Not unless you want to hike for about three days up the mountain." Ben stood with his hand on the roof of the shuttle. He'd pulled on a black jacket, but he still wore his light blue uniform. "You can't be afraid of flying. How did you get out here?"

"He's not afraid," Tegwin said. She dug into her pocket and handed Luis a few plastic-wrapped disks, striped red and white. "Luis gets terrible motion sickness."

"Why didn't you tell me?" Ben started back toward town. "Wait here, I'll get you something."

"That's okay, Ben." Luis smiled at Tegwin, hoping he

didn't look too green and sick already. "Nothing I've ever tried works. I think I've tried everything ever invented already."

Ben put his hands on his hips, shaking his head.

"You haven't tried everything, because you've never been to Bitanthra before. If you think you can make it, we'll go on now. But let me just see what I can do for you when we get back."

"You got it," Luis said. "I'm willing to try just about anything. Fly as smooth as you can, and I'll warn you before it's too late."

Ben did the best he could with the small craft, and he kept up a running narration the whole time to help Luis concentrate. The exploration of the planet and the discovery of Bitan. The story of his family's arrival on Bitanthra, getting the original mines set up and running. His own experience working in ore processing and sorting before he switched to medicine.

Luis focused on the landscape and Ben's voice, clenching and opening his fists. The shuttle climbed smoothly up wooded slopes covered with an unbroken canopy of soft-leaved trees. The forest shifted as they climbed higher, getting more steep and rugged.

Jagged grey outcrops broke through masses of deep green pine trees, the tallest Luis had ever seen. The trunks and branches were covered in mats of fluffy moss in every shade he could imagine. The shuttle passed through cloudbanks, covering the windscreens in mist and huge drops of water.

"How you doing, Luis?" Ben said. "We're about five minutes out."

"I'm okay," Luis lied. "Just keep talking."

He gripped the seat, clenching his teeth as the shuttle turned, a long, slow bank to the right.

"I'm sorry about that." Ben glanced at Luis. "We have to

stay in approved flight paths once we get this high. See the ore shuttles up ahead?"

Luis popped another of the mints into his mouth, breathing in the sharp aroma. A line of slow-moving, massive versions of the craft he, Tegwin, and Ben were in ranged along the ridgeline.

All the transports moving to the left were full to the top of the precious Bitan, obviously green even from a few hundred meters out. The line heading to the right were all empty.

"They load up at the mouth of each mine," Ben said. "Then head back to the big storage areas in the valley. When it's been a while since a TransG freighter has been here, it looks like you could make another mountain out of the Bitan piled up there."

"So they may not miss a couple of pieces." Luis tried to smile.

"They'd miss it," Tegwin said. "Even with that much, the loads are weighed down to the milligram."

Ben brought the shuttle in low under the line of transports, heading to a flattened space on top of the mountain. A cluster of stone buildings in regular rows took up most of the space, surrounded by a ring of shuttles of various sizes and shapes.

"TransGalactic headquarters for this region," Ben said. "A few families live up here, and a bunch of the miners stay during their work shifts. We'll find Dad here while they're loading up the *Bountyfield*. Guaranteed."

Luis waited for several seconds after Ben landed, eyes closed, willing his stomach to behave. When a strong gust of wind swayed the blocky shuttle, he took his chances and climbed out.

Ben stepped between Luis and Tegwin, shoulders hunched against the hard breeze.

"It never stops blowing up here. Just stay close behind me. Everyone else should be out working right now, so we won't have to dodge folks going off-shift."

Luis stared up at the huge transports as they walked under them, marveling at how the gigantic craft could possibly be so quiet. He counted at least thirty strides to cross the shadow of one.

"This is really a short crew up here today," Ben said, raising his voice over the wind. "Most everyone is down in the valley loading."

"It takes over a month to load the *Bountyfield?*" Luis said. His belly finally felt calm, and the sweat was drying on his face.

"No big freighter had been out here for a couple of years," Tegwin said. "The next one is already inbound. An extended break in the Bitan supply chain would be a disaster for more than TransGalactic. All the AlliedSystems would be in trouble."

Ben stopped outside the first building at the edge of the field, a two-story stone house with edges so sharp Luis thought they might have been laser cut.

"Dad can be a little bit hyper-focused at the start of a big load. Let me get him talking, get his attention. Then you can jump in. He really is a great guy away from all this."

Luis hummed to himself as soon as they stepped inside, trying to straighten his hair and clothes after that driving wind. Several desks were scattered around the quiet, dark-walled space, everyone focused on meter-wide plas-screens in front of them.

"Ben, what brings you up here?" A tiny woman, barely as tall as Ben's chest, walked from behind the desk closest to the front door. "You know Dad's impossible to talk to when this mess is going on."

"Don't I know it. We have a couple of visiting doctors

from TransG here on assignment. I wanted to make sure they see what we do out here in the back end of nowhere. Luis, Tegwin, this is my sister Anna Lee."

"Glad to meet you." Anna Lee gripped Luis's hand harder than anyone else on Bitanthra had. "This will be the best thing for him, really. Make him focus on something else for a minute so he'll relax."

Luis laughed, making sure he didn't look at Tegwin. No matter how high up Ben's father might be in the chain of command, trying to convince anyone to let them wander off with a near-priceless chunk of Bitan wouldn't likely make them relax.

"We'll do our best, ma'am."

Anna Lee flashed a crooked smile, a perfect miniature version of Ben's. She knocked on the broad wooden door beside her desk and opened it before Luis could think of what he was going to say.

## Chapter 14

THE OFFICE WAS MUCH SMALLER than Luis expected, less than half the size of the room they'd just walked through. There was barely space for a sleek, black desk, several shelves stuffed full of photo-screens and printed books, and a few leather chairs.

The man standing behind the desk was medium height, unlike his towering son or petite daughter. Mr. Essena had a slender comm unit in his hand, and a spherical holo-reader, much larger than the one Luis carried, floated above the desk. Luis caught a glimpse of multiple moving documents, each full of charts and numbers, before Mr. Essena killed the display.

"Ben! What a nice surprise," The two men hugged, thumping each other on the back and smiling. "Taking a break to visit your old dad in the middle of the day."

"I know, I know. It's been a while. Work actually has been busier than usual lately. This is Doctor Luis Ahmad and Liaison Tegwin Fairbrooke. They're here from TransG, looking into what's been going on with our children."

"Mike Essena," he said, shaking Luis and Tegwin's hands.

"I'm glad they're finally taking our trouble here seriously. Without our families, nothing runs on Bitanthra. Without Bitan, the whole galaxy doesn't run. Please, have a seat."

"I know how busy you are right now, Dad, so I'll get right to the point. Luis works with deep psych-hypnosis, trying to figure out what's going on. This morning, they were able to get through to a couple of the Becalmed."

"Did you find out what's been causing this?" Mr. Essena said, leaning forward in his chair. "No one else has had any luck so far."

"We're still not sure, no," Luis said. "We got emotional responses they've never had before, responses that seem to affect the brain as well. We think the difference might be the Bitan in these bracelets."

Mr. Essena blinked and drew back.

"There's hardly any in those things."

"That's what I thought," Tegwin said. "But as soon as Luis put his on and started work, everything changed. Mine increased the effect. Their brain patterns and everything shifted. Even without that, we had no doubt they were upset."

"Upset, huh." Mr. Essena rubbed his smooth chin. "Two of my grandkids are Becalmed. Much as rowdy kids like Ben and Anna Lee can be a handful, it's heartbreaking to watch them pull away like that. You think you have a cure?"

"We're not sure yet," Luis said. He paused, trying to guess what the right words would be. "The next thing we need to try, that I'd like to try, is working with more Bitan. Larger pieces. I'm hoping that would amplify the field more than these bracelets do."

Mr. Essena smiled, but he was already shaking his head.

"You've never been here before, have you?" He tapped the holo-reader, and the moving documents popped up again.

"See all this? These are tracking the big load going on right now, down in the valley."

He tapped the side of the sphere, bringing up another set of displays.

"These track the mining operations up here on the mountain. At all times. TransGalactic is a wonderful company to work for, treats us very well. But they track every gram and molecule of Bitan. I don't know what they think we could do with it, or why we'd want to. No one sells or installs it in tech but them. I doubt they think we'd do anything at all, to tell you the truth. Still, they don't take any chances. The stuff is too valuable."

"Sir, this could solve the problems you've been having here," Tegwin said. "Help get the colony stabilized and keep it that way. I'm quite sure TransGalactic would be nothing but grateful."

"And they told you this?" Mr. Essena said, shutting down the displays. "When you asked about the Bitan?"

Ben held out both hands, palms up.

"You know better than I do how long they take to do anything. If we asked for authorization through them, the *Bountyfield* would be long gone, and Dr. Ahmad with it, before they ever make up their minds."

Mr. Essena looked from Luis to Tegwin and back again, tapping his fingers on the desk. The comm unit buzzed, making Luis jump. Mr. Essena glanced at it, then frowned.

"I'm truly sorry to disappoint you, but this isn't possible. Certainly not right now, with the TransGalactic flagship over our heads. One thing Ben might not know is they don't just weigh or count Bitan. Not anymore. They track the molecular signature."

He stood, and the others stood a second later.

"Anyone planetside and everyone up on the *Bountyfield* knows the supply won't hold out forever," he said. "Nothing else works the same way. Without it, communication is impossible across systems. They're planning to bring in automated scouting shuttles in a couple of years to scour the mountainsides and the paths under those big loaders. Trans-Galactic needs every grain of Bitan, and they're going to find it. I'm afraid you'll have to work through them on this."

"Thank you for your time," Luis said.

He was already running through his schedule for the next few years, wondering what he could bump to stay or return to Bitanthra. With the hypersleep journeys arranged so far in advance, it could easily be several years.

He'd have to find someone else with deep psych experience, see if they could rearrange their schedules. Or see if TransGalactic would let him adjust his caseload instead.

Tegwin interrupted his gloomy train of thought.

"Yes, thank you," she said. "May I ask how many grandchildren you have, Mr. Essena?"

Ben's father smiled, his mood instantly shifting.

"Five so far. Three girls and a boy. Two more on the way, which will have to do until Ben here makes up his mind about that girl he's been dating."

Tegwin smiled, and reached out to shake Mr. Essena's hand.

"That's lovely, congratulations. I understand your position about the Bitan, sir, I do. But I have to tell you, the rate of children born Becalmed has increased since TransGalactic last released information. It's passed fifty percent now, and still climbing. I hope you can see your way clear to help us as soon as possible. May I reference you in my official request?"

Mr. Essena shook himself.

"Of course, please do. I'll do everything I can, Liaison Fairbrooke."

## Chapter 15

No one spoke until they were nearly back to Ben's shuttle. Luis stared up at the transports over his head, so vast and slow they seemed to hanging still. He couldn't stop himself from watching the ground under his feet as they walked, hoping for one of Mr. Essena's stray chunks of Bitan.

"So you'll file your request with TransG," Luis said. "Then we'll see how long it takes? Any chance they could come through sooner?"

Tegwin shook her head. "We're not exaggerating how slow they are, Luis. They're locked into long-range thinking, which they have to be in a way. They started construction on the *Bountyfield* ten Earth years ago for this specific trip. It's booked for at least the next thirty-five years already. Probably more after these meetings."

"And if this colony collapses in the meantime?" Luis saw the school kids, walking in endless circles instead of playing. "That won't get them moving any faster?"

Tegwin glanced at Ben, and Luis was surprised to see he was smiling.

"Go right ahead, Tegwin," he said. "I have no illusions about how this place works."

"If the colony collapses, or before it does, really, Trans-Galactic would bring in other workers. They don't want to, we talked about this. Production costs would skyrocket with much higher salaries, and constant transport and training time thrown on top of that. But even with all that, Bitan will keep moving."

"Have they considered how fast the Becalmed population is growing?" Ben said. He wasn't smiling anymore, but he didn't look nearly as upset as Luis felt. "How fast it's really growing?"

The nurse leaned against the shuttle, and Tegwin stepped close to speak above the roaring wind.

"Are you telling me it's higher than fifty percent now? The numbers I updated just a few days ago?"

Ben crossed his arms.

"I'm telling you it's jumped fifteen percent in the last few months. If it goes on at this rate, we'll be at seventy-five before the end of this Earth year."

Tegwin's face paled, and she held one hand over her heart.

"Why haven't you-"

"Reported it to TransG? We have. When you took up orbit. Around the same time you got your update, right?" He waited for her to nod. "Now I don't know if this is just their normal glacial pace of operations, or if they've decided to let the colony fail instead. If I had to guess, I'd say they weren't expecting those numbers. Otherwise they wouldn't have bothered bringing Luis and his expensive equipment all this way."

"They rearranged my schedule," Luis said. "Bumped or reassigned several cases to get me here. I was just now trying to figure out how we could manage to do that again so I could stay."

"How often do they rearrange *any* schedule?" Ben said. "For any reason? They're wanting to save this place if they possibly can. I'll sign on to your request, Tegwin, and I know a few other people who will as well. Obstetricians, teachers, folks like that. We'll see if that gets their attention."

They all got settled in the shuttle, and Luis opened his last mint. He wasn't quite recovered from the ride up.

"Why did you ask my father about grandkids, Tegwin?"

"I thought…I hoped if I put it in those terms, he might be willing to help us. I think he wants to, don't you?"

"I know he wants to. He asks me about it a lot, that's why I suggested coming up here. What he didn't tell you is one of those babies is due in just a couple of weeks. No one on Bitanthra wants this figured out more than he does."

Luis managed to hold out until they arrived back in town, with the return ride much smoother and faster. But he had to detour into the brush before they walked back to the medical facility.

"Don't you leave here without letting me get something for you," Ben said. He still had a small smile, and he acted much less worried than either Luis or Tegwin. "You might be surprised at what all grows around here."

"Whatever you have, I'll try. Can I ask you something?"

"I told you, that's what I'm here for."

"Tegwin and I were talking about the temperaments of most Bitanthrans. How some of them might be a little more emotionally reactive than typical humans. Does that sound right to you?"

Ben snorted. "We deserve our reputation as a rowdy bunch if that's what you're asking."

"I know you've all been concerned about the Becalmed

and that getting worse. Has the rest gotten worse too, more intense?"

Ben rubbed his chin, exactly the same way his father had.

"I'm not really old enough to remember, just in my late thirties Earth Standard. But there were stories when I was off-world doing my medical training. People talking about how Bitan made us a little crazy. I was just a kid and didn't pay much attention. I thought they were just picking on us because we're such a small, rural colony."

"Would there be any kind of records we could look at?" Tegwin said. "Medical or maybe school records?"

"You think this is related?" Ben said.

"I don't know how it could be," Luis said. "But we don't know what causes any of this yet. I don't want to rule anything out. No matter how TransGalactic handles our Bitan request, I'm here for a few more weeks at least. May as well use the time."

"I'll see what I can dig up. Do you have any data for that, Tegwin?"

"No, but I have been coming here for a long time. Longer than you'd believe with hypersleep. I think the population is changing, too."

Luis pulled out his small comm-screen. "I'll get started writing up the data we have so far for your request, Tegwin. I'll check my schedule for the next few years, then work out a testing protocol for Bitan. I'm not giving up until I have to."

## Chapter 16

Luis nearly missed a step when they rounded the corner toward the medical center. Two people stood in front of the door, a woman and a man. Both had their arms crossed, and neither looked happy.

"Myrtle and Wills," Ben said. "I'm guessing they've spoken with Helen and Drew."

"And they're not going to want to speak with me," Luis said. "Or maybe they do, but I'm not going to like it."

"They didn't have any trouble with their testing, did they?" Ben glanced at Luis. "I can head them off, but it would help if I knew what I was walking into."

"They didn't get as upset as Helen did this morning," Tegwin said, slowing her pace. "I'd say Myrtle got a bit upset with her first psych field."

"I don't think she's happy about any of this," Luis said.

"They're scared," Ben said. "Like the rest of us. Let me see what's going on."

The two leaders stepped forward and uncrossed their arms, but neither of them were smiling.

"How are you two doing this afternoon?" Ben shook

hands with both of them. "I was just showing our guests the Bitan operation in action."

"We're fine," Myrtle said. She never took her eyes off Luis. "I was hoping Luis and Tegwin would join us for lunch this afternoon. Fill us in on how their work is going."

"We'd be glad to," Tegwin said. "What time?"

Willis stepped forward. "We can have everything ready by the time you wash up and meet us at our house if that works for you."

"We'll be there," Luis said. He tried to be optimistic about the invitation. At least they hadn't yelled at him out here on the street. "Just give us about ten minutes."

"See you there." Myrtle inclined her head, then they both walked away.

"Should I be worried?" Luis said when Ben closed the medical center door.

"I don't think so," Ben said, with that same little smile. "Just be honest with them. That's all most people want, especially when it comes to their children. Tell them the truth and do the best you can for them."

"That I can promise."

The table wasn't quite as stuffed full as the first time Luis had eaten with Willis, barely an hour after leaving the *Bountyfield*. There was more than enough food for four people, but not enough for twice that many.

His solitary dinners from the food stores in his apartment had been filling, but not especially satisfying. He was thankful the conversation was light and pleasant enough so he could enjoy the meal after his stomach's rough morning.

The respite didn't quite last until the last plates were cleared.

"So tell us, Luis," Myrtle said, leaning back in her chair, "what have you learned so far with Helen and Drew?"

Be honest, Ben said. Might as well take that advice.

"We had a bit of a surprise this morning. When we activated the psych field, they both had emotional responses. Helen didn't seem to care for it, but I think Drew was curious."

Myrtle glanced at Willis, and they both nodded. First test passed, Luis hoped.

"Helen stopped by here after they finished up," Willis said. "She wasn't pleased, no. Is this some kind of cure? What do you think made the difference?"

"It's too soon to call it a cure." Luis thought of Helen's cold, stony eyes. "Helen has no desire to be like us. She made that quite clear."

"She told me the same thing," Myrtle said. Luis caught the faintest trace of a smile. "She said if we all walk around a mess inside like that, it's no wonder we're always fighting and crying and carrying on."

"She has a point," Tegwin said. "I had a brother and a sister, and our teenage years were nothing but drama."

"Why are you not calling it a cure?" Willis said. "For the ones that want it, or for the young children? Sounds like this would help them."

"It might," Luis said. "We don't know how long the effect will last, or if it would cause some other kind of problem. With the adults, I'm afraid of slamming them into emotions with no time to adapt. Both Helen and Drew had strong reactions, a bit above typical to be honest."

"Where were Willis and I on that range?" Myrtle said.

"A bit high a couple of times. When I asked you about what was causing the numbers of Becalmed to grow, for instance."

"That's going to set most of us off, I believe," Willis said. "I'm not surprised we're above normal, either. If you're thinking it *could* be a cure, what do you need to do next?"

Luis looked at Tegwin, and she shrugged. This was probably the place in the whole galaxy where Bitan was the least secret.

"We think these comm bracelets made the difference." Luis held up his wrist. "The ones TransG gives permanent staff like Tegwin, or people on assignment for them, like me. But the amount of Bitan inside is so small."

"We were trying to get a larger sample," Tegwin said. "Up by the main mine. They weren't able to help us, so we're going to make a request to the *Bountyfield*."

"They track every speck and scrap up by those mines now," Myrtle said. "Not like when we were younger."

Luis stared at her, afraid to speak. Tegwin did it for him.

"When you were younger? Are you saying someone in town might have larger pieces?"

"You expect me to answer that question from a TransG liaison?" Myrtle said, amusement clear in her voice. "We've heard how strict they are about it now, how they're gathering up all the stray pieces they can find."

"Doubt they'd pay what it's worth, anyway," Willis said. "Even to the ones who mined it for them."

"I can't pay anyone," Luis said, trying to keep his voice calm. "I don't have any local currency. Even if I could access all of my galactic credits, I don't have nearly enough for the speck of Bitan in this bracelet, much less what we'd need."

"What *do* you have, Luis?" Myrtle said. "What can you offer us?"

"I can offer to do my best to help your children. Adults too, if they want it. Anyone who lets me use Bitan for this, I can promise I'll give it back. There's no possible way I could sneak it onto the *Bountyfield*, anyway."

"How long do you think you'd be waiting for that official request to come through?" Willis said. "TransG wasn't exactly fast last time we tried to get anything changed here. We plan for months and expect years."

"They're the same," Tegwin said. She had her hands knotted tightly in her lap, obviously as anxious as Luis was. "Weeks would be a miracle."

"And you'll be gone by then." Myrtle nodded to herself. "Well, the best we can do is think about it, maybe talk to a few people. I can't make any promises. I doubt anyone I know actually has any. But you answered our questions, and that means a lot to us."

"That's all I can ask," Luis said. "If Helen or Drew are still willing to work with me, I'll do my best for them. You too, or anyone else who wants to help. I'll do my best."

## Chapter 17

Luis rubbed his achy eyes, trying to get the numbers and data in front of him to stop blurring. He'd been in the exam room for hours working on the report for Tegwin. He normally had days to dig through, especially when writing up a treatment or experimental protocol.

He didn't want to delay this project by even one minute if he could help it.

The truth was he had more than enough to justify for a return trip to Bitanthra, probably with a few technicians and all the equipment he needed. The results from Myrtle and Willis's single deep psych field were almost as interesting as the Becalmed.

Older long-term memories stored the same as most humans. Average distribution throughout the brain, some stronger with more emotional ties than others. The more recent memories, though, within the last thirty Earth years, were anything but average.

The newer long-term memories for both were stronger, deeper. Nearly enough to reach traumatic levels for typical humans. Too many at that level for people living on a peaceful world.

Something was changing here, at least for Myrtle and Willis. Working with more subjects was no longer a nice idea Luis would pursue if he had more time or more sensors. He had to bring in more people, downloading and resetting the sensor nets daily if necessary.

The tiny grain of Bitan around his wrist might just have to do.

Luis was staring at the exam beds, wondering if he could risk a quick nap without falling asleep for hours, when someone knocked.

Ben opened the door when Luis called out, a huge grin on his face.

"What are you doing here so late?" Luis glanced at the time on his notescreen. "What are you doing *awake* so late?"

"Well, I had an urgent comm from my dad. Seems he's been in touch with some of his old friends down here, pretty much nonstop since we left. He still can't send us any Bitan from the mine, so don't get your hopes up about that."

"I've got plenty to study while I'm still here," Luis said. "Maybe with our three bracelets, we'll see a difference."

"Sure, we can do that. But you might want to come see what was out front waiting for me."

Luis stretched as he stood, groaning at the crackles in his back. He'd been sitting there way too long. His sluggish mind finally caught up with what Ben said by the time he got to the nurses' office. A shade was pulled in the window, blocking the view out to the lobby and the street.

"They sent Bitan?" Luis stared at the pile of packets and envelopes, even one gleaming wooden box bigger than his two hands. "Myrtle and Willis?"

"No idea, and that's the way they wanted it. Dad didn't

tell me anyone's names. All they ask is we put all of it back in the same containers."

"How much is all of this worth?"

Luis picked up the box, marveling at the multi-colored inlays and intricate metalwork.

"I doubt we could price some of these in galactic credits," Ben said. "I've never seen this much outside of the mines. I'd imagine once TransG gets around to sweeping the town, all of these will be gone unless we can work out something with them. So everyone keeps them well hidden."

Inside the fabric-lined box were two pieces of Bitan, each as big as Luis's fists. He held one up, surprised at how heavy it was.

"They had enough to carve them. It's beautiful."

The dark, pine forest green surface was polished to a glasslike finish, forming a rounded cube. Grooves a few millimeters deep made swirls, lines, and spirals, each fiery with flashes of jewel tones as Luis turned the Bitan.

"No one was really sure what they had here," Ben said. He picked up the twin to the one Luis held. "Carved ones like this go back to the very first colonists to arrive, before TransGalactic got involved."

"I can't tell you how much this means to me, Ben."

"You can show me, Luis. Me and everyone else. I'll get you all the subjects you need, give you support staff if you need us. Help us figure out what's going on with our kids."

Luis nodded, not sure he could speak.

They carried the Bitan back to the exam room and unpacked it all, arranging the pieces in a row in front of their containers. The samples ranged from a few millimeters across to the two in the box, all carved or at least polished.

The treasured reminders of the first residents of Bitanthra might end up saving future generations.

"You're asleep on your feet, Dr. Ahmad," Ben said.

"Everything is ready here, and it sounds to me like you have more than enough written up for Tegwin's official request. I'd guess she might appreciate a little company, too."

"Yeah, we probably should still do that request, huh? If they do come through, I can get these back to their owners a lot sooner. We need to start with these smallest pieces, I think."

Ben spoke from right behind Luis's ear.

"Luis! Put the screen down. Go back to your room and get some sleep. Better yet, go join your liaison and tell her I said the same goes for her."

The nurse was smiling, but Luis knew better than to ignore that tone of voice from anyone.

"I'm going, right now. You heading home?"

"I'll catch a few hours in one of the other guest rooms. I'll have a stimulant waiting for you in the morning. We're both going to need it."

# Chapter 18

LUIS HAD NEVER BEEN one to underestimate the comfort of sleeping beside another person, especially one so compatible with him. Tegwin had indeed still been awake and more than willing to take Ben's stern advice. The few hours Luis managed did more for him than an entire night on his own.

Ben was explaining to Tegwin how they ended up with enough Bitan to pay for their own *Bountyfield* by the time Luis staggered into the exam room the next morning. Both had already finished their own stimulant drinks, and Ben handed one to Luis without interrupting his story. The earthy, steaming hot beverage cleared his thinking as soon as he swallowed it.

"Taking these from the families would be a crime." Tegwin held a slender piece of Bitan as long as her hand, carved with symbols in a language Luis didn't recognize. "Just as much as from any of the indigenous populations back on Earth or anywhere else."

"We hope that's how TransG sees it someday," Ben said. "But for now, we keep these hidden. Most of us don't even know who has what. I sure didn't. Dad might tell me someday if he ever decides I'm grown up enough."

"I'd never even heard rumors about them," Tegwin said. "Not in all the times I've been here. I think you're right about submitting the official request anyway, Luis. You know I was up half the night working on it too, so we might as well."

"I have a basic testing protocol ready." Luis activated his screen and sent the documents to Tegwin and Ben. "If anyone shows up to let us test. We may have to take you up on your offer of more subjects."

"Dad said he was going to talk to a few people," Ben said, heading toward the door. "I think Myrtle and Willis will too, after all the conversations flying around town last night."

"Is this going to cause you problems?" Luis said after Ben left. "With TransGalactic?"

Tegwin stepped into Luis's arms, then turned to gaze at the row of Bitan, shaking her head.

"If they ever find out I knew about this and didn't tell them, maybe. I'm serious about these staying here. I don't have a lot of influence over cultural issues, but my brother worked with creating settlement procedures on a few colonies when he was first starting out. He might know how we could go about doing that here."

"You ready for this?" Luis brushed her red hair back from her face, resisting a strong urge to kiss her. "Assuming anyone shows up?"

"This is all new to me," she said, laying her head against his chest. "Deep psych field was only a theory when I finished my training. Are you ready?"

Luis broke away and walked in a circle around the exam beds, adjusting everything for at least the tenth time since the previous afternoon.

"This is outside anything I've ever done or read about. We could help save this colony, the culture they have here.

Or, we could prove that it can't be saved. Most of the time I'm trying to help individuals, you know? Not save an entire colony."

Ben opened the door enough to peek through, his usual bright smile firmly in place.

"Your first four subjects are here."

"Four?" Luis turned to Tegwin. She shook her head. "Bring them back."

The door opened wide, and Helen and Drew walked in, followed by Myrtle and Willis.

"I didn't think…I'm so glad to see all of you!" Luis said, not sure if he was about to laugh or cry.

"We all had a good talk last night," Myrtle said. "What you're doing is the best chance we've had to figure out what's happening here for a long time. Since the trouble first started, really. We at least want to do our part."

"We can get started right now," Tegwin said. She held out her hand toward the exam table. "Unless any of you have questions."

Helen and Drew both nodded and stepped forward.

"Your promise still holds, Luis?" Helen said. "I know you might not be able to fix what already happened. But you'll try not to change me if you can help it?"

Luis took her hand, helping her onto the table.

"I promise. Thank you for your trust. How are you feeling, Drew?"

The Becalmed man smiled, the expression more natural than Luis would have believed two days ago.

"I admit I was scared yesterday. I know more what to expect now. I think I'd be fine if I get changed a little more."

"Perfect. A test and a control. Exactly what we need. Do you think you can get your sensor net on, Helen? That way we won't get too close to you with the Bitan bracelets."

She nodded, and she had herself set up and ready before

Tegwin and Luis were finished connecting the net and the table's other diagnostic sensors for Drew.

"What we'll do is take a quick scan to see how your brains are looking today." Luis touched the skull-shaped sensors, waiting as maps of Helen and Drew's brains lit up the interiors. "You can watch these if you want, Myrtle and Willis. The scan will give us a basic idea whether the changes are lasting. Then if all goes well, we'll try Drew with the deep psych field."

Neither of the Becalmed's brain maps had changed overnight, which was what Luis expected. He had no idea what to expect with the next part of the test.

"Okay. Your brains look the same as they did yesterday. The effect is lasting so far, and it's not progressing on its own. If you're ready, I'll activate the deep psych field. Then we'll see how Bitan affects Drew."

Luis touched the sensor temples, then held his fingers over the top of each skull.

"Starting field in three…two…one." He tapped the top of each skull. "How are you feeling, Helen? Same as yesterday?"

"I'm the same. Still have a mixed up spot inside my head, but it's not as bad."

"Drew? How about you?"

The Becalmed man had his eyes closed just like Helen, but his face was more tense. His eyes were squeezed closed, his mouth drawn up.

"I feel about the same. The truth is I want you to try to change me. I liked what happened yesterday. I thought about it all night long."

Luis looked at Myrtle and Willis. When they both nodded, he waved Tegwin forward.

"We're going to try only the Bitan in these bracelets now. Not for you, Helen, only for Drew."

They held the silver bands on either side of Drew's head. He took a deep slow breath, but his body didn't draw up like it had before. Myrtle and Willis leaned down to peer through the skull sensors.

"I'm seeing a few changes in brain waves," Luis said. "No new points in the brain map yet. What do you feel, Drew?"

"Warm in my belly, churning around. I feel like I'm wide awake."

"Good." Luis picked up two of the smaller pieces of Bitan, giving one to Tegwin. "We're trying larger pieces now. You can tell me to stop anytime you want to. Remember that."

They held the ore around Drew's shoulders, then gradually moved closer. The movement of his brain waves intensified, making deeper peaks and valleys. His heart rate and respiration increased as well.

"Chest feels tight," Drew said, shifting his arms and legs. "Muscles, too."

"I'm seeing increased activity that may be anger," Luis said. "Try breathing deep like you did before, then blow out the tension with your breath."

When Drew's vital signs were closer to normal, Luis and Tegwin moved the Bitan to beside his temples.

"If you're comfortable, I'm going to ask you a few questions," Luis said. "Some of what we did yesterday." He waited for Drew to nod. "Do you know what makes you Becalmed, Drew?"

"Too much coming in. More than we can stand. Hurts too bad."

"Too much coming from people around you?"

"No. From far away. Another place. Bad things, bad people."

Luis looked up at Myrtle and Willis.

"Do you know what he's talking about?"

They both shook their heads, brows wrinkled.

"Helen, you can hear what Drew's saying," Luis said. "Does that sound right to you?"

"That's how it felt yesterday," she said. "When you changed my brain. Like something outside could get in where I didn't want it."

Myrtle pointed at the skull showing Drew's brain map. A few new red dots glowed, more scattered than the day before. They were almost as big and intense as Myrtle's strong long-term memories.

"We're going to try bigger pieces of Bitan now, Drew." Luis let Willis take the smaller bits of ore and give them larger ones. "I want you to keep thinking about that place far away. See if anything gets more clear."

Drew clenched his fists, and Luis saw his thigh muscles tighten.

"Is this going to hurt him?" Myrtle said. "Hurt his brain?"

"All these sensors have warnings built in," Luis said. "The brain does what it can to protect itself. One big way is drawing blood in from the limbs. If his hands or feet get cold, or his heart rate gets too high, we'll know we need to stop."

"I want to keep going," Drew said. His fists were still clenched, but he was smiling. "I like the way this feels."

"You're doing really well," Tegwin said. "Can you tell anything more about the far away place? I know the Becalmed don't dream all that often, but do you think it's somewhere you dreamed of?"

"Some kind of trouble. Secret. No one talks about it." He paused, his forehead and mouth wrinkling. "I don't think it's a dream. Doesn't feel like here. Doesn't feel like in my head. Don't dream much, though. I hope I dream more when I'm changed."

"Maybe you will," Luis said. "Rest for a minute, Drew. You too, Helen. We're not going anywhere, just taking a break."

He activated the white noise dome over the two of them and waved everyone else over.

"Is it possible the Bitan is doing more than amplifying their emotions?" he said. "I know this might sound irrational, but it does enable faster than light communications across all the known systems."

"You reminded me that we don't have any idea why they're Becalmed," Tegwin said. "They've lived their entire lives on a planet full of Bitan, with mountains of it moving around on the surface. I'm not ready to rule anything out."

"I've never heard of anything like this, though," Myrtle said. "Sending a voice or data with Bitan is one thing. But thoughts? Feelings?"

Luis stared at Myrtle, her first deep psych running through his mind. People didn't always remember what they said when they were under.

"Do you remember what you said about this, Myrtle? Under the field? Lots of times people can't. More often than not, really."

"You mean about poison? I do think that's what it is, without any kind of field."

Tegwin shook her head. "You said it felt like it didn't come from here. Like it came from far away."

Myrtle sighed and crossed her arms.

"No, I don't remember that. I suppose you have everything recorded like you told us, or else you wouldn't have said so."

"I do. I'm not trying to cause trouble or make you feel bad. But like Tegwin says, we can't rule anything out just yet."

"What does that mean?" Willis said. "If it is something like that, what could we do about it?"

"That's a whole bunch of steps ahead of me," Luis said. "I don't think I'd know where to begin, anyway. If this is some kind of broadcast, I hope Tegwin would know what to do."

Tegwin laughed, raising one eyebrow at Luis.

"I hope you're not serious. First thing I'd do is ask for help. How can you even begin to verify some kind of external broadcast?"

Luis stared at the row of Bitan along the wall without seeing it. Saying he was working beyond his training and experience didn't even come close.

So far, anyway, he was beyond his imagination.

"Well, right now we have two people who've said a problem, a poison, is coming from far away. Under deep psych hypnosis. No one has ever been able to lie when they're under the field. The first step in verification is recreation."

Myrtle squeezed her lips so tight that they disappeared.

"You want me or Willis to try it again. See what happens with Bitan this time. Right?"

Luis nodded. "It is voluntary. I don't mean volunteer or else, either. I'm not going to coerce you or make you feel guilty. I've love for both of you to try. And, if you don't want to, that's the end of the discussion."

"Is it going to change us?" Myrtle said. "Like it is Helen and Drew?"

"We haven't tried any typical Bitanthrans with Bitan yet," Luis said. "What I'd do is verify your scan from the first day, then we'd watch while you're under. I can stop if I see any changes, or I can ask what you want to do if it happens."

Willis held out his hand to Myrtle.

"Let us talk about this for a couple of minutes," he said. "You can ask Helen and Drew some more questions, right?"

"Absolutely." Luis grabbed his discarded comm badge

from the work table. He'd been so excited when Tegwin gave him his official comm bracelet that he'd forgotten all about it. "You can use this to get into my room, or Ben can let you into another one."

"I think the hall will suit us just fine." Myrtle took Willis's hand and followed him out.

"A transmission," Tegwin said. She rubbed her upper arms. "That doesn't sound like a pleasant one to get."

"No. If it's true, we'll have more questions than answers. And no easy way to deal with any of it."

"Typical day around here, Dr. Ahmad. Let's see what else these two have to say in case Myrtle and Willis agree to let you tinker with their brains."

Luis stopped the white noise, then sat beside Helen.

"What's happening with you, Helen? Do you have any sense of trouble coming from far away?"

"I still feel like I can't reach it. Today I don't feel like it can reach me. That's safer. Better."

"Okay, good. We only have one more question for you today, since you're the control. You're one of the leaders of the Becalmed. Do you think many of you would want to be changed? If you could?"

"A lot of people want us to change. Our families sure do. But I don't think many of us want to. We don't want to leave our home, or cause everyone else to have to leave. But most of us like the way we are."

"I'll make sure everyone knows that. One last question for you, Drew. Do you mind if we try a little more Bitan?"

Tegwin handed Luis the long, slender piece he'd seen her with earlier that morning. She held its near-twin.

"Go ahead."

Luis and Tegwin moved the Bitan wands closer, watching Drew's vital signs. This time his brain activity increased, but his breathing and heart rate stayed normal.

"He's adapting so fast," Luis said under his breath. "Drew, I want you to think about that far away place. You'll still be safe here, but do you think you could feel more of it? Like opening a window?"

Drew was silent for a long moment.

"I think I could open the window and I'd know more. I'm afraid, though. Feels like a dream there, a bad one. The dreams that scare regular kids."

"A nightmare." Tegwin shivered. "Adults have those, too."

"It might be a nightmare," Luis said. "I want to ask Myrtle and Willis about this first, since they've had nightmares before. Then we may ask you again."

"Will you let me try, too?" Drew said. His heart rate increased a little, and his cheeks flushed. "Let me look through the window? I want to see a new place even if I never leave home."

"Of course, Drew." Luis glanced over as Myrtle and Willis came back in. "You can open it as wide as you want to. We'll make sure you're safe. Okay, I'm bringing both of you out of the field in three…two…one. Helen opened her eyes in a calm face, as if she'd just woken up from a nap. Drew was smiling again, his eyes bright and merry.

Luis no longer recognized the Becalmed man he met a few days ago. He hoped Drew understood others in his community may not, either.

**Chapter 19**

MYRTLE LEFT no doubt about who was in charge as soon as Helen and Drew got to their feet.

"We'll help you, Luis, or at least I will. From what you tell me, I got a stronger sense of something coming from outside of Bitanthra than Willis did. Mine was more like Drew." She looked at Willis, and he nodded. "I'd feel better if Willis stayed awake. I know that sounds like I don't trust you, but I wouldn't be here if I didn't."

"Of course, we can do that," Luis said, trying to keep up. "We'll do whatever makes you the most comfortable."

She turned to Helen and Drew.

"I know you two are leaders of your community, and all of this affects you directly. But I need you to leave while we're doing this. I'll feel a lot more comfortable."

Drew shook his head and started to speak.

"No, Drew," Myrtle said. "Don't forget I'm older than you. This is medical treatment, right?"

This time Tegwin gathered her wits in time to respond.

"We do classify it that way, yes."

"Then I have every right to privacy." Myrtle touched

94

Drew's shoulder. "We're not trying to hide anything from you. I have a feeling this isn't going to be easy is all."

Drew scowled, but he let Helen take his arm and walk him out of the room. Myrtle sat on one of the exam tables.

"Now let's see what you can figure out."

Luis returned Tegwin's half smile as they both jumped to do Myrtle's bidding. He sat beside her when the sensor net and monitors were all in place.

"We'll get the field established, then start with the smaller pieces of Bitan. I know you have a lifetime of experience with emotions, Myrtle. But if this gets too strong or feeling out of control, you can tell me to stop. Promise me you will?"

She stared at him, gaze steady but eyes narrowed in fear.

"I promise, Luis. If it is too bad, you can treat me for trauma or something like that, right?"

"I can. I don't want to get to that point, though. Your brain activity is normal, so we're ready. Starting field in three…two…one."

Luis and Tegwin each held the smallest pieces of Bitan close to Myrtle's head. The intensity of her brain waves increased, but her vital signs stayed level.

"Focus on what you felt before," Luis said. "The sense of poison from outside Bitanthra."

"Feels like a light shining," Myrtle said. "Or music from a long way off."

They switched to larger pieces of ore.

"That's louder. Stronger." She shifted her back and shoulders. "No one knew this could happen. But no one can figure out how to make it stop."

Tegwin pointed toward Myrtle's skull sensor display. Luis didn't see any new dots, but some in the amygdala were glowing brighter to match her increasing brain activity.

Fear. And anger.

"Drew talked about opening a window," Luis said, taking

one of the Bitan wands from Tegwin. "Do you feel like you can do that, Myrtle? Or maybe pull the feelings closer to you?"

Myrtle took a long, slow breath, but her heart rate increased.

"Hidden away. No one knows they exist. No one wants to know."

"Do you have any sense of what kind of place it is?" Luis said. "A planet, a moon? A ship, maybe?"

He and Tegwin held the Bitan wands alongside Myrtle's head, nearly touching her temple and jaw. She shifted her legs, then spread her fingers wide. Movement she shouldn't have been able to manage under the field. Just like Drew.

"I feel trapped, deep under the ground. Cold, dark. Not like I'm supposed to be. So many there. So many…"

Tears rolled down Myrtle's cheeks, cutting through the sweat.

"You're starting to show signs of physical distress," Luis said, watching her breathing and heartbeat. Both were getting faster. "We can pull you back now, take a break."

She shook her head, squeezing her eyes tight.

"No break. Not yet. Lost and terrified. I don't want to leave them there."

She held out her hand, and Willis took it in both of his. Luis saw tendons stand out on her wrist, her fingers sinking into Willis's flesh.

The fear levels in her brain waves were near the top of normal ranges, but her breathing and heart rate slowed. Luis's own heart jumped at the concentration of red around Myrtle's fear centers.

"Can you find anything about them, Myrtle? Any bits of language? We can't normally read thoughts with deep psych, but we've never gotten emotions from another mind, either."

"The outsiders bury them, put them away. Like they're not real at all. If anyone finds out, they would have to leave."

Luis's stomach turned over even though he was sitting perfectly still. He knew the horror stories from early colonization days. Everyone who worked for TransGalactic did. It seemed humans didn't behave much differently when they moved to new planets as when they'd moved to new continents on Earth centuries before.

"Do they feel human to you, Myrtle? Can you get any sense of that?"

Her whole face crumpled and she turned her head away. Her voice was strained, forced through a tight throat.

"Monsters. Humans are monsters. Kill us instead. Kill us all."

"Can you try to send to them?" Luis said. "Whoever you're in contact with? Try to let them know we're going to help them, to hang on?"

Myrtle's body tensed, and Luis heard the first pinging alarm from the bed's monitors. Her hands and feet were getting colder.

"I can't find them. We can't help them if I can't find them."

"Listen to me." Luis held his hand over the skull sensor, getting ready to stop the field. "We know you can contact them, at least two of you can. I think they must have Bitan, so they have to be a wealthy colony. We *will* find them, Myrtle."

She shivered, and Luis heard her teeth chatter. Myrtle drew in a huge, great breath. As she let it out, her brain activity peaked, then started to decline.

"Hang on," she whispered. "We'll find you. We'll find you."

Myrtle opened her eyes as soon as Luis ended the field.

"Did I just lie to them? You said we *couldn't* lie under the field. We can't possibly find them when we don't even know where to start."

Luis turned to get a blanket, but Tegwin already had one. They tucked it around Myrtle as closely as they could, but her temperature was already coming back up.

"Something as valuable as Bitan will be tracked, Myrtle." Luis hoped it was the truth. "Anyone who can afford it can't stay hidden forever."

# Chapter 20

Luis closed the door to his apartment and leaned against it, rubbing his temples. The same spot that primed the deep psych field on the skull sensors. He wished he could instantly activate the same focus and calm inside his own stormy brain.

Ben and Tegwin had helped get Myrtle and Willis settled in to another of the guest quarters, then checked on Helen and Drew in theirs. All the Bitanthrans were fine as far as Luis could tell. Vital signs normal, resting comfortably. They were all understandably wary of doing more, but hopeful that they could help figure out whatever was going on.

Underneath all that, Luis could see Drew was trying to hide his growing excitement. For a man who'd never dealt with emotions at all, much less how to hide them, Luis thought he was handling the rapid adjustment quite well.

Luis didn't feel like he was doing well himself. Not at all. He'd had the door closed for all of five minutes, and he was already regretting his own suggestion that he and Tegwin take a break. Alone. Maybe sleep for a little while, let their minds sort through and figure out what to do next.

His mind was only spinning faster and faster, his heart and gut joining in the chaotic motion and distress.

He walked into the kitchen and held his hand over the drinks spigot, with no clue what he should dispense. A light sedative, enough to let him relax but not quite sleep? A stronger one to knock him out for a few hours and settle his whirling thoughts? Or the strongest stimulant in the kitchen's programming, one that would overpower his late night and send him careening into another?

Luis settled for apple juice instead, grown and pressed in sprawling orchards not far outside of town. The fruit was as crisp and tart as any Earth apple he'd ever tasted.

Cold glass full of amber liquid in hand, he abruptly decided staying in his apartment when he couldn't sit still for more than a few minutes didn't make sense. At least he could get outside, walk around in the cool, foggy air.

He nearly dropped the glass when he opened the door to see Tegwin raising her hand to knock.

"You too?" she said, smiling. "I'm going to lose my mind if I try to sleep. You didn't sound like you wanted company, but maybe you want to with me?"

"I was just heading outside, and I very much want your company. I haven't really taken advantage of having the planetary liaison for the Bitan homeworld by my side. I might ask you a bunch of questions."

"I'll be driving you nuts asking how we can combine Bitan and deep psych for people who aren't from Bitanthra soon enough. If it amplifies the field for everyone, we may solve more than one problem on this visit."

Luis swallowed the last of his juice, managing to set the glass on the counter without breaking it.

That was what his mind had been endlessly circling, just out of his reach.

"Maybe we can try that out right now," he said. "If you're willing."

Tegwin leaned against the kitchen wall with her arms crossed. Luis was relieved to see her eyes held more challenge than caution.

"You want one of us to try it. Going under the field."

"It's a logical next step. At least while everyone else is resting. We'll know a hell of a lot more about how this works, how much effect the Bitan has for people from anywhere but here. We might even be able to locate where the signal's coming from."

Tegwin shook her head slowly.

"We don't even know what we're looking for. What kind of life it is. We may be able to see if Bitan changes things, sure, but how could we locate anything?"

Drew spoke from just inside the open door.

"I'll help. I want to. I'm not going to sleep any time soon, either."

The spark in Luis's chest, his clear hint he was about to zero in on the solution, flared hot.

"We can try," he said. "But do you have any idea how to direct me? Where it came from?"

"No." Drew stepped into the apartment, his eyes bright and excited. "I know how it felt, though. Can't we both go under the field together or something? Maybe Myrtle can help us since she's used to emotions."

Luis rubbed at his face.

"That's not…No one does that outside of training. And only then, after all subjects have a good idea of what they're doing. It can be dangerous, Drew."

"Dangerous how?" Drew said. "More than changing my mind into something new? Or dangerous to you?"

"Well, to both of us, really," Luis said. His mind was already running through calibrations and setup, getting two mapped brains into the same field. Three if Myrtle was willing. "We don't have an instructor here to monitor us, for one thing. One or the other of us could get into trouble. Any of us. Mental or physical, if the field gets out of balance."

"I can monitor you," Tegwin said. "I've been in on how many sessions now? You keep talking about how advanced and automated the systems here are, Luis."

Luis wished he'd gotten out the door for that walk before the conversation went this far. And he wanted to try Drew's idea.

Right now.

"I just want to help them," Drew said, his voice soft. "Whoever they are. Whatever they are. If we just find out *where* they are, maybe we can. Maybe TransGalactic can."

"If it means saving this colony," Tegwin said, "TransGalactic will do whatever it takes. Come on, Luis. What do I need to know that the diagnostic systems here don't already monitor? That you don't know yourself?"

Luis leaned against the counter, tapping his fingernails against the cold stone. She had a good point. Once TransGalactic finally saw a clear reason to get involved, to throw all their resources behind a problem, they finally did move quickly.

That could be the best, fastest way to save Bitanthra and whoever was sending the signal.

"Okay, we'll try it," he said, walking toward the door. "We'll see if Myrtle is willing to help us, that's a good idea. But I'm setting parameters on the monitors and on the bed's diagnostics. This whole thing stops if any of us get into any trouble."

Tegwin bowed her head and waved her arm.

"Lead the way, Dr. Ahmad."

## Chapter 21

THE SETUP WAS FINISHED LONG before Luis was ready, or at least before his nervousness overcame his excitement. It was a simple matter of adjusting the connections, the communications, between three of the sensor skulls and nets. Instead of connecting one to one, all sets now worked in parallel. The fourth stood ready to display the combined data as needed.

Tegwin, Drew, and Myrtle watched every change he made. They all asked questions, and Tegwin made notes the whole time. Luis didn't mind the attention, knowing explaining as he went would act as a backup. If he could teach it, he could do it correctly.

Ben sat between the exam beds with three of the oval data pods in front of him. He'd hesitated, but only long enough to work out the safety protocols with Luis. He was nearly finished changing the settings.

Helen sat beside Willis in front of the row of Bitan. Neither had tried to argue with Drew or anyone else, but they'd insisted on watching.

"Pay attention to how this is going to work," Ben said,

waving everyone over. "The alert levels are higher, or lower in some cases. The big difference is instead of just an audible and visual alarm, these are connected to the deep field emulator now. If you hit more dangerous levels, the panels will cut the field."

"What if we don't want that?" Drew said, scowling. The expression still looked strange on the man's youthful face. "I wanted to keep going after the alert, and you told me Myrtle did too. I don't want that machine to cut me off if I almost know where they are."

Ben glanced at Luis. Myrtle nodded, but she didn't look as distressed as Drew.

"We have to be careful, Drew," Luis said. "This is a first-rate medical facility, one of the best I've ever worked in. I'm including my training days in that. But one reason is so you can have less staff here, right, Ben?"

"He's right. We're so remote it can take weeks to get specialized help. Years in the case of someone like Luis. They handle the most serious injuries to the miners on the orbital med station. So we have as much automated down here as we possibly can."

Luis nodded. "That helps us, and Ben is an excellent nurse. If we run into real trouble, though, we'll be on our own. We can call out for assistance, sure. But we can't take too many risks, Drew."

The Becalmed man put his fists on his hips and stared at the ground. His cheeks were red, and his voice trembled when he spoke.

"I just don't like everything automatic like that. Can't you fix it so Tegwin can override it, or you, Ben?"

Tegwin touched Drew's shoulder. He twitched, but didn't move away.

"I'm going to tell you something I'm really not supposed to. I'm pretty sure you already know, though. The reason the

Becalmed don't work in the mines or any other dangerous operation is because you don't seem to have fear. Without that, you can get into a life-threatening situation that you wouldn't otherwise. Or put other people into danger even when you don't mean to."

"We do know that," Helen said, her voice barely above a whisper. "We don't want to hurt anyone."

Drew looked up at Tegwin. He dropped his hands to his sides.

"We could get you under the field to ask you this," Tegwin said, "but I'm hoping you'll just tell me the truth. Do you think you've changed enough to be afraid for your life, Drew? Afraid for your mind?"

The Becalmed man sat heavily on an exam table, holding his head in his hands. Luis watched his shoulders rise and fall slowly, but he could hear those breaths. He would have bet a year's salary what Drew was going to say.

Luis would have won that bet.

"That's the part I don't like out of all of this," Drew said. "I'm scared to *death* most of the time. Every shadow makes me jump at night, every breeze and noise. My chest stays tight and my muscles hurt. I keep thinking about bad things that could happen to Helen and Myrtle and Willis, and to all of you. I'm afraid this part will keep getting worse. I'll be too fearful to even leave my house."

"I think a lot of that will get better," Luis said, standing in front of Drew. "Lighter, easier to deal with over time. You might not remember this, but when you were under the field, I asked you to take in a deep breath and blow out, like you were letting some of the anger pass through you. Can you try that?"

Drew breathed in, his chest hitching a few times, then breathed out in a loud hiss. He looked up at Luis with tears standing in his eyes.

"I feel a little bit better. How'd you know to do that?"

"Our bodies are every bit as involved with emotion as our brains are. You have to learn how to work with the physical responses to help with the emotional ones. And, I knew because I have decades of practice. That's all."

Luis sat on an exam bed, taking his own deep breaths.

"Can you please put in an override, Ben? So you or Tegwin will have to make the choice to stop the field?"

Tegwin stared into Luis's eyes, then Drew's and Myrtle's. Myrtle sat on the third bed, nodding again.

Tegwin shrugged and turned to Ben.

"Go ahead. They all look scared to death to me. That's probably right where they should be."

She helped with their sensor nets, then helped Ben activate the monitoring on all the beds. Luis had already explained everything that was different about the dual field, but he couldn't stop himself from going through it again.

He knew he'd be eternally grateful to Tegwin and Ben for listening instead of telling him to shut up.

"This will take both of you. Start the brain mapping for each of us. Once that's done, start the fourth sensor. Then you can activate the deep field. The fourth sensor will coordinate and show you what's happening, what's matching up among us."

"Will do," Tegwin said. "We'll keep watch over all of you. If you get into trouble, I'll use that override without hesitation."

Drew rolled his eyes, but he smiled at Luis. Humor added in now. They couldn't properly call him Becalmed, not any more.

"Starting the mapping," Ben said.

Luis tried to relax against the exam bed, which was every bit as comfortable as he'd imagined. Every part of his body felt cradled, weightless.

He wished his mind felt the same way.

"Baseline established." Tegwin turned the monitor so Luis could see it. "Drew's brainwaves aren't that different from yours now, and Myrtle's are a little higher. Any last advice?"

Luis tried to laugh, but his throat was too dry. He wanted to help the mysterious source of the signal, and he wanted to help the Becalmed. Even if that meant leaving most of them as they were and preventing more from being born to save the colony.

He wasn't sure he wanted to experience the nightmare that led more than a generation of Bitanthrans to block their emotions as some kind of self defense.

"Remind me that Drew and Myrtle are taking the lead at first," Luis said. "Then remind them to let me be in charge once in a while, too. Don't get too close to us, either. People usually don't move under deep psych, but that's another rule out the window."

She nodded, a half smile on her face. Luis's belly filled with heat far beyond a simple mission pairing. If he came through this deep psych with his mind intact, his heart was going to be in trouble.

"Safe journey, all of you," Tegwin said. "Starting field in three…two…one."

## Chapter 22

THE PHYSICAL SENSATIONS of Luis's body faded away, one after the other. His back against the soft exam bed. The chilly air against his hands and face. Clothing, from his shirt and pants all the way down to the weight of his shoes. He knew he'd struggle to move his body right now if he tried, even though the Bitanthrans had managed.

His sense of smell increased, bringing in Tegwin's familiar scent, a lingering wood fire from Ben, and some kind of pipe Willis probably smoked at least an hour ago. His hearing did the same, picking up everyone's breathing and the smallest movements. His eyes were already closed.

He knew most of that would fade away just like his body's feelings had. The only thing that lingered by design brought Tegwin's voice.

"All of your readings look good. I'm entering the sequence to bring Luis and Myrtle into the field together. Then we'll add Drew if all goes well."

Luis focused on opening his brain, as if he could physically pull down the barrier of his skull. The feeling increased until a tingling sensation moved throughout his mind, spreading slowly through his body.

He forced himself to breathe deeply through increased fear, and greatly increased anger. If these were normal levels for Myrtle and the other typical Bitanthrans, it was no wonder they had such a fierce reputation.

"Both of you still with me?" Tegwin said.

"Still here." Luis heard Myrtle say something along the same lines.

"Your emotional readings are up, Luis, but not at critical levels. Be ready in case Drew brings in a whole lot more. He's coming online now."

Luis gasped before he could stop himself. This time it wasn't just fear and anger that jumped, though those spiked white hot into his head and chest. Joy, dread, impatience, amusement, even lust surged through him. He hadn't been such a hurricane of emotion since he was a young teenager back on Earth.

"Everything just jumped," Tegwin said. Luis tried to control a burst of desire for her, hoping his body didn't respond without his permission. "How you doing, Luis?"

"I'm fine. Trying to hang on. We'll have a lot more training and adjustment with Drew once we're done here."

Luis thought he heard Myrtle mutter something like good before all of his attention turned to something new. Something alien.

"Picking up a new reading," Luis said. "Maybe our signal."

"Myrtle, can you focus on what you felt before?" Tegwin said. "Drew, can you do the same?"

The faint sensation, like a whisper in another room, turned up loud and clear. Luis couldn't find one clear feeling, one clear being, to hold on to. His mind plunged into a million shifting bits of sand.

"So many," Luis said. "All at once. Is that what you're feeling?"

"Too many to count." Myrtle's voice was soft and airy. "Nothing to grab hold of."

"Can you bring Luis closer?" Tegwin said. "Show him more?"

The *many* sensation intensified, prickling all over Luis's flesh. He thought his arms and legs shifted, but it was too distant to catch.

"Can't get closer," Drew said. His disappointment raged through Luis, nearly bringing him to tears. "Not like before."

"We're going to try Bitan in a second," Tegwin said. "Take a few breaths for me first. Try to calm that response before we go deeper."

Luis realized he was breathing hard and fast, and he was sure his fists were clenched. A giant pit of agonizing heat tore through his middle. Certainty that they'd never succeed, no matter how hard they tried.

He heard Drew and Myrtle breathe when he did. One, two, three times.

"You're doing great, Drew," Luis said, trying to convince himself. "You too, Myrtle."

"You all are," Tegwin said. "Bringing the Bitan toward you now."

Luis's mind *jumped*, propelled at unknowable velocity and distance. The many feeling resolved, turning from sand into countless tiny bubbles. The abrasive scratching disappeared, but now he was drowning in terror and fury.

"What…what are you?" he whispered, pushing the words out through his mind. "What happened to you?"

Whispering, like rain in a forest or the white noise field, filled his head. Luis couldn't find a single word or thought to hold out of billions.

"More Bitan," he said, not sure if his voice was loud

enough to cut through the whispering. "Need a stronger field."

"Going up one size." He recognized Tegwin's voice, but she sounded underwater. "Watching your brain levels, though. Getting close to red."

Luis sucked in air as he was pushed forward again, and this time he knew Myrtle and Drew were with him. He could feel them, the color and shape of their thoughts.

One whisper grew louder than the rest, and he realized he could hear thoughts.

But not from Drew or Myrtle. These didn't feel remotely human.

Each word, each syllable came from a different consciousness. Luis felt his brain struggling to translate raw emotions into words.

*Trapped. Terrified. Dark. Forgotten. Buried.*

"Who are you?" Tears rolled down his cheeks. "How can we help you?"

*Bury us more and more. Don't even know we're alive. Invisible. Unseen. Draining our life away.*

Luis's chest and stomach felt crushed, pressed in from all sides. The bubbles he'd sensed earlier boiled now, abrading him worse than the sand ever could have.

"Help me reach toward them," he said in a rough voice. "Find something we can recognize."

"Find the anger." Myrtle's voice boiled the same as Luis's flesh. "The fury. This way."

The pressure and scraping intensified into heat, heat that felt like Myrtle and finally like Drew. Luis slipped into the raging current, leaving all of his training and experience and civility and humanity behind.

He was all fire and rage and velocity, compression and suffocation and darkness.

A piercing noise jerked a sliver of his awareness back. The brain activity alerts he'd insisted Ben set.

"That's it, all three of you are in the red." Tegwin's voice spiraled and twisted, touching Luis and floating away. "Dropping the field in-"

"No!" Three throats, one voice, one mind. "Almost there!"

A low, grinding ping, repetitive and harsh, joined the singing alarm.

"Okay, that's my monitors." Ben. Warped and fluttery, nearly impossible to grasp. "Body temperature dropping, along with heart rate and respiration. Time to cut it."

"More Bitan, please," Luis said, begging Myrtle and Drew to help raise his voice. "One more push. Let us find them. They're running out of time!"

Luis had no sense of time to tell how long Tegwin delayed. Anywhere from a nanosecond to millennia were the same to him. He and Myrtle and Drew within still sang with relief when she spoke.

"Turn up the heat in the room, Ben. On the beds, too. You have one minute, Luis. Less if I hear one more alarm. Make it count."

Luis wasn't sure if he spoke with his throat or only inside his mind.

"Drew, you have to lead us. Don't be afraid, don't hesitate like we would. Throw us. Throw us as hard as you can."

The clammy, shadowed cloud of fear shrank down to nothing, replaced with a glowing blue shower of pure joy and enthusiasm. Luis felt himself contract along with Drew and Myrtle, shrinking far past where their bodies could have fit, beyond where their conscious thoughts could exist.

The three of them slipped into a stream of that darkening blue, shading into green, pressure behind them building with explosive force.

Beyond wind.

Beyond water.

Beyond the speed of anything but light.

They shattered into a consciousness as many as the stars, as the atoms in the galaxy, the universe.

Branching out together, linking through the land and sea and stone. Making up the solid ground, the earth that sustains an entire world.

They weren't on that soil, or even in it.

They *were* that soil, every particle and molecule.

"Tell us how to help you. How to find you."

*Stop them crushing us. Forcing us to suffocate and die. Draining the life away from us, drop by drop.*

"Extraction. Water. Something. Destroying life they don't even know is there."

The fury Myrtle led them to shifted, changed, faster than Luis could react. Shock to fear, faintest hope to brightest exultation.

The touch of Myrtle and Drew dissolved into a multitude, amplified into the frantic grasp of recognition.

*You see. You feel. You are here.*

Luis's voice, his thoughts, echoed and rebounded far more than he and Myrtle and Drew could have ever imagined.

"We can find you. We'll stop them hurting you. We have to go now."

The answering shriek sent Luis recoiling, slipped the tiniest strand of nerves back to his body.

He heard the last alarm braying impossibly far away.

"If we die back there, no one will ever find you. Remember my voice, all our voices. Let us go so we can help you."

Desperate pulling, wanting to shred them away from their fading bodies. Resistance Luis could not fight holding all of them. Drowning them beside the billions they'd finally found.

Myrtle screamed forward, her rage and joy magnificent as it was terrifying. Luis leapt into her.

Taking the rage as his own.

Following the blinding path she blazed.

He could only hope Drew followed.

## Chapter 23

Sensation returned in an agonizing flash.

Luis heaved and gasped, trying to remember how flesh and bones and lungs worked after an eternity away. He squeezed his eyes shut against the glaring lights, tried to draw away from the overheated air on his drenched skin.

"Luis! Cut the field, Tegwin, now!"

Someone touched his forehead, hands cool and soft against his flesh.

"The sensors cut it a few seconds ago," Tegwin said. "See how Myrtle and Drew are doing. Luis? Back with me?"

"Almost. Can't work out how to breathe yet."

"Same way you always have." She touched his chest and his stomach. "In and out. Sounds like you found something."

Luis concentrated on the gentle pressure of her hands, pushing down, relaxing. He heard Willis talking to Myrtle, and Ben and Helen talking to Drew.

"Something, yeah. No idea what."

"Tell me before you forget." Tegwin cupped his cheeks with her palms. She spoke over her shoulder, reminding the others to ask the same question. "The recording is still going, and I'm not letting you or anyone else go through that again."

Luis did the best he could, talking even as the surreal experience faded from his mind and body.

"Extraction," Tegwin said. "Water, or something like petrol, maybe?"

"I'm not sure about that part. They felt like, well, like they were part of the planet. Part of the earth, the soil. Anything on the surface or under it could feel like extraction to them. I know this whole thing sounds nuts, and I'm afraid it doesn't help us much with finding them."

Tegwin smiled, looking sideways at Luis, the glance that melted his heart right before he went under. She handed him a warm mug, instantly taking possession of the rest of him.

"What part of this whole mission hasn't been at least out of the ordinary? You happen to know someone with access to TransGalactic's records. Planetary liaison and all. I'd say we need to start about thirty years ago, from when the first Becalmed were born."

Luis swallowed all the stimulant at once, groaning as it drove the last chills from his fingers and toes.

"This place could have been colonized for decades before that. There have to be dozens of new colonies in all that time. Hundreds."

"I'm sure there are. But we know exactly when every one of them went online with Bitan. That's an instantaneous connection, remember? And an expensive one, not available to a small or failing colony, especially so long ago. That cuts the numbers considerably."

Drew stood, holding on to Helen for a second before he walked to Luis's bed. He looked far more stable than Luis felt.

"I think we'd recognize them," he said. "Don't you? The way they feel, what they say."

"Maybe. Only if we talk to a person planetside, though. I don't want to do that again."

"When can you have the list of colonies?" Myrtle said. She was still on the exam bed, Willis sitting with his arm around her. "So we can get started?"

"I'll start the search in the morning," Tegwin said. "Ben, you told us anyone in town would be happy to feed us. If you can find someone to handle this whole group, we'd certainly appreciate it. No arguments. Nothing else happens until everyone gets a good night's sleep."

## Chapter 24

Tegwin's low voice dragged Luis out of a dreamless sleep, deep enough that his stiff arms and legs told him he hadn't turned over all night. Not since he and Tegwin had finally fallen asleep, at least.

The trouble he'd sensed had bloomed full force throughout his heart and mind as soon as he held Tegwin's warm body to his own. Weeks away from the end of this mission, and Luis was already dreading the separation. He hadn't made the mistake of getting overly attached since his first couple of pairings decades ago.

Light from the wrong side of the bed confused him for a moment. Everything was reversed in the tiny space. Seating area, kitchen, front door. He didn't remember going into Tegwin's apartment rather than his own, but the pile of TransGalactic blue bags rather than his black ones confirmed it.

She sat by the small round kitchen table by the windows, holo display activated in front of her, note tablet in hand. Instead of talking to someone on the comm like he'd thought, she was muttering to herself.

The scent of fresh coffee coming from the huge mug on the table brought Luis all the way into consciousness.

"Good morning." He sat up, stretching his back. "How long was I out?"

"About ten sweeps, same as the rest of us. Want coffee?"

Rather than answer, Luis grabbed his robe from the foot of the bed and walked into the kitchen. He poured a mug for himself with equal parts coffee and Ben's stimulant drink, then refilled Tegwin's cup.

"Find anything?"

She turned the tablet toward him as she took a long drink.

"Fifty-seven colonies came online with Bitan within our timeframe," she said. "Several were lifeless worlds, no more than rock with a rudimentary atmosphere. I've pulled out thirty-three as likely targets for our signal."

Luis scrolled through the list, wondering if some kind of new sense would alert him to the right one. If it was, he was missing the signal.

"I'd guess there will be some kind of biomass," he said. "Existing long before any colonists arrived. A form we may not recognize as sentient."

"From what all three of you said, I expect it will be diffuse. A hive intelligence, even more so than Earth ants or honeybees."

Luis sighed, rubbing his arms.

"That's still a lot to try to sort through without throwing ourselves out there again."

Tegwin grinned, then walked to the food prep pod. Less than thirty seconds later, she sat a plate in front of Luis. Light brown toast, applesauce, and the delicious scrambled chicken eggs he couldn't get enough of, all at the perfect temperature.

"There are a few more secrets planetary liaisons keep

from the general public. You know how the larger pieces of Bitan amplified your deep psych field? They work the same way with communications. Most ships, comm units, and colonies hold the smallest amount needed to get them onto the network. A flagship like the *Bountyfield* holds considerably more."

"That can't make the signal faster," Luis said. "It's already instantaneous."

"No, not faster. Stronger, though, able to carry a much heavier signal with more information. Multiple channels in simultaneous use. You never notice the limitations until you operate through one of the bigger arrays. I suspect we can adjust that signal, make it diffuse enough to target an entire colony instead of the comm links."

Luis took both of her hands in his.

"And you have the authority to make that adjustment, my dear Liaison Fairbrooke?"

She squeezed his hands and shrugged.

"Not directly, no. I was just finishing an emergency addendum to our official request. Between that and the recordings from last night, I'm hoping TransG responds a lot more quickly than usual."

"Everyone else gave permission? Myrtle and Drew did?"

"Last thing last night, right after you crashed. Ben sent the notice over before I had a chance to ask."

Before Luis finished his breakfast, Tegwin's comm chimed through. She switched the external sound on before answering.

"Everyone appropriate in there?" Ben said, and Luis could hear the smile in his voice.

"Appropriate and mostly alert," Tegwin said. "Everyone else good this morning?"

"We're great here. In fact, we'd appreciate it if you'd join us in the nurses' station. We've had some developments this morning that you might be interested in."

Luis thought about crossing the hall to his apartment for a change of clothes, but something in Ben's voice kept him from taking that much time. The last time the nurse had summoned Luis, it had been for a room full of Bitan worth more than most planetary incomes.

Ben waited with Myrtle and Willis, Helen and Drew. If anyone noticed his robe, no one said a word. A video comm was displayed on the large central screen, with the Trans-Galactic logo front and center.

"We're ready here, *Bountyfield*," Ben said, speaking toward the screen. "Please replay the command message for Dr. Ahmad and Liaison Fairbrooke, then we'll stand by."

The blue and gold logo dissolved, revealing Ben's father and a woman Luis didn't recognize. She wore a TransGalactic command uniform, like Tegwin's but decorated with various symbols and several gleaming metallic insignia. Her age was impossible to guess as part of a hypersleep fleet, but her short hair was more silver than black.

"Commander Holbruck," Tegwin whispered. "Chief of the Deep Space Fleet."

"Good morning," Commander Holbruck said with a nod. "I've been briefed on the progress of your mission, Liaison Fairbrooke and Dr. Ahmad, including your official request. Director of Mine Operations Essena joined us today with most interesting recordings from a recent group psych-hypnosis session."

She turned to Ben's father.

"I believe these recordings will allow us to better understand and address the risks to ongoing Bitan operations," he said, "and more importantly, to the stability of our colony. All of us on Bitanthra and throughout the AlliedSystems express our gratitude for your efforts so far, and our hopes of moving forward."

"After careful consideration," the commander said, "I'm directing TransGalactic to put all necessary resources at your immediate disposal. We await your response."

After several seconds of silence, Luis laughed out loud and caught Tegwin in a hug. Everyone else joined in, with Drew louder and more boisterous than the rest.

Only Helen stood to the side, a tiny smile on her face.

"You did it," Luis said. "We all did it! How did you get your father to go up there, Ben?"

"We had a chat last night is all. He's up half the night whenever a freighter's loading anyway. Once he heard the recordings, he asked for those and all our other data. I didn't know he was going topside until this came through a few minutes ago."

"Speaking of topside," Tegwin said, jerking her chin at the screen. "Commander Holbruck, ma'am. Director Essena. Thank you for your attention and quick response."

Luis fought the urge to run back to his apartment, settling for pulling his robe closer to hide more of his sleep shirt. His spiky, messy hair would just have to do.

"The possibility of a decades-long violation of a sentient species is too serious to send through normal corporate channels," the commander said. "Whether the settlers are aware of the problem or not. What do you propose, Liaison?"

Tegwin pulled her comm tablet out and touched the screen.

"Sending our emergency addendum now, ma'am. I've gathered a list of possible colonies, all coming online within the required timeframe. I propose adjusting the Bitan array on the *Bountyfield* to a diffuse target of the entire planet, and transmitting while subjects here are under the deep psych field."

"Not the same field as last night?" Ben's father said. "Sounded to me like you were in physical distress."

Tegwin turned to Luis, eyebrows raised.

"No, sir," he said. "With the assistance of the larger array, we should be able to employ a normal field. Assuming our subjects here agree?"

Drew grinned, stepping forward beside Luis. He bounced on his feet, like he was struggling not to jump toward the screen.

"Yes sir and yes ma'am. I'll do anything I can to help Dr. Ahmad."

Myrtle smiled and nodded, and Willis did the same at her side.

"Helen?" Ben said, holding his hand out to the Becalmed woman.

She waited against the wall for a long moment, staring at the screen. She finally stepped between Ben and Drew, but she was shaking her head.

"I'm sorry. I can't. I want to help, I do. But I don't want to change any more than I already have. I want to stay Becalmed."

"We won't force any of you," Commander Holbruck said. "Every citizen of Bitanthra will make their own choices in this delicate matter. We all thank you for your efforts to save your colony."

Helen nodded and slipped into the background again.

"I'll review your proposal, Liaison Fairbrooke," the commander said. "And bring the Bitan array chief and crew in to consult immediately. Everything sounds reasonable at the moment. We will have to operate within a tight schedule with our array offline, at the chief's discretion. Please be prepared to act quickly during that timeline."

"Yes, ma'am," Tegwin said. "Thank you both."

When the screen went blank, she turned to Luis. Her kiss

fired his chest and every other part of him into full, vibrant life.

"Ready to work up another protocol, Dr. Ahmad?"

"As fast as I can write it."

# Chapter 25

FOR THE FIRST time in his life, Luis went through planetary deceleration without a trace of complaint from his normally unruly stomach.

The passenger transport vessel *Zortea* was nowhere near as vast or as new as the *Bountyfield*. But as the passenger flagship for TransGalactic, the *Zortea's* accommodations were more comfortable and luxurious.

Rather than huddling in the lowliest crew quarters, Luis relaxed in one of the spacious VIP recovery suites. The bedroom was larger than his apartment back on Bitanthra, with a warm air suspension bed and fragrant thermal baths and shower.

He'd been unable to resist combining earthy patchouli with sharp pine in his bath, trying to recapture the air of the Bitan homeworld. Much to his surprise, he enjoyed the results enough to record the recipe for future use.

Part of Luis resisted all the decadence, thinking back to the rock-hard bunks and solid metal walls that had seen him through countless queasy re-entries over the decades. He didn't actually need plas-screen walls set to preview each environmental zone of the destination planet, scenes from a distant homeworld, or anything else the occupant desired.

The foggy mountains of Bitanthra surrounded him at the moment.

He could certainly get by without mood-sensing crystalline lighting from Outer Rigia, or ambient music tuned to his waking bio-rhythms.

Luis also knew better than to argue with TransGalactic when they insisted on providing such posh accommodations. And he had to admit he'd miss them on future missions now that he was able to enjoy the experience. He had at least a few years before he had to worry about that.

He'd left the polished wooden door open, so he heard movement in the dining area beyond. After a lifetime of hypersleep travel, Luis and his growling stomach were looking forward to his first expertly prepared recovery meal from the best chefs in any fleet in the galaxy.

The scent of coffee mixed with Ben's stimulant brew finally got Luis moving. He savored the way his toes sank into the thick Tafeya-fiber rugs, how the lighting shifted from warm reds to brighter blues as he moved.

The suite's airlock door was just closing as Luis entered the dining room, and his heart leapt at the sight of Tegwin waiting for him. She sat on the far side of a huge round table laden with dishes and bowls all covered with copper, gold, and silver domes.

She wore a green version of his purple Kayren silk robe, the color setting off the red tones in her hair perfectly. Luis felt like he hadn't seen her in far longer than the six years of hypersleep.

"Good to see you, Director Ahmad."

Luis caught her in a long hug and a peppermint-flavored kiss. The intense, fiery connection forged between them in the last weeks on Bitanthra hadn't waned at all from his perspective.

"Good to see you, Director Fairbrooke. Do your duties as head of diplomatic relations for the Gosijune System still include briefing a lowly psych officer on changes while we were in transit?"

"Only for the head of tele-psych operations. Everyone else will have to find an overworked and underappreciated planetary liaison."

"If they've assigned any yet," Luis said, sitting beside her. "Have the colonists agreed to resettlement terms?"

"Everyone who wanted to leave has already gone. All ground-based infrastructure has been removed, restoring the ground cover and bio-mass to their original states."

She bit into an orange fruit with pink flesh held in one hand while changing the dining room's plas-screens with the other. A lush, tropical world replaced Bitanthra's rocky land-scapes. Thick beds of blue moss surrounded lower, flatter areas taking on paler shades of the same coloration. In the distance, towering black and purple plants ringed the open space.

"The Gosijunes are recovering," she said. "Slowly but surely. A few of those trees are sprouting in the more temperate zones. The polar ice caps are receding too, getting back to their original size. As far as we can tell, that's still the only area on the whole planet where their colony organism hasn't penetrated."

"How did TransGalactic set up landing ports?"

"Turns out as long as our hover platforms move enough to allow the entire surface to get sunlight, the Gosijunes do just fine. We have a system of twenty landing ports and thirty residential bases so far. The orbital facilities bring the total accommodations up to nearly five thousand."

"And Bitanthra?"

She smiled and laughed under her breath. Luis hoped they'd have a little time alone before it was time for the drop to the surface. Once they'd finished eating, of course.

"Drew is bursting with wanting to talk to you. He's been in nearly constant contact with the Gosijunes. His emotional training went wonderfully. Ben says he'll always be exuberant and sometimes a bit moody, but he's handling all of the changes himself now. He's actually expecting his second child with a typical Bitanthran woman. Ben's expecting his third."

Luis shook his head, trying to imagine Drew staying calm while keeping up with toddlers and later teenagers.

"They'll both make wonderful fathers. Sounds like the birth rate is recovering."

"Back to normal levels. Before the Becalmed."

"How's Helen doing? Still their liaison?"

Tegwin paused long enough to finish her stimulant-coffee mix and pour herself another.

"This is wonderful stuff. I'll have to put in for a bonus for Ben. Helen is still the Becalmed liaison, yes. To tell you the truth, I think she's a little sad that no more were born once we made contact with the Gosijunes. Sad as she can be, anyway. She's doing a great job coordinating the ones who want deep psych treatment."

Luis helped himself to a second serving of loretfish lox, the perfect balance of spicy and sweet too good to resist.

"Double that bonus for Ben with my authorization. Thanks to him and his magic herbal brew, I finally under-stand why people eat so much after hypersleep. How many of the Becalmed are seeking treatment now?"

"Looks like it will stabilize at around thirty percent for any level of treatment. About a quarter of that stops at the mild adjustment Helen has. Seventy percent end up in the middle ranges. Only five percent go as far as Drew and full emotional restoration. He's convinced more will return for higher levels once they get to know him better."

"He's probably right." Luis watched the plas-screen shifting to an arid region covered with fuzzy mats of brilliant yellow growth. He was afraid of the answer to his next question. "How long will your assignment here be, Tegwin?"

She stared into her bowl of steaming tri-grain porridge for several seconds.

"Setting up a new diplomatic outpost is quite different from a run of the mill liaison mission. This won't be a typical outpost either, not with the coordination of Gosijune telepathy and the Bitan network. We'll be assisting with your tele-psych training program, too, scaling that up once you develop the protocols."

She ducked her head and looked sideways at Luis, melting his heart all over again.

"How does four years sound?"

"Like we're about to land in paradise."

# ABOUT KARI

Kari Kilgore's wanderlust and imagination lead her all over the world on grand adventures. Her heart and family bring her home to her native Appalachian Mountains of Virginia. From that solid base, she and her husband Jason A. Adams bring those adventures to life in fiction.

Kari writes science fiction, fantasy, and horror, and she's happiest when she surprises herself. She lives at the end of a long dirt road in the middle of the woods with Jason, various house critters, and wildlife they're better off not knowing more about.

## The Confidential Adventure Club

For Kari's exclusive free After The End stories and deleted scenes, discounts, early pre-sale releases, adorable pet photos, and a whole lot more not available anywhere else, visit The Confidential Adventure Club at www.smarturl.it/c-a-club.

Hope to see you there!

www.karikilgore.com
www.spiralpublishing.net

## ALSO BY KARI KILGORE

I hope you enjoyed reading *The Becalmed* as much as I enjoyed writing it. Check out more of my fiction at www.karikilgore.com.

### The Confidential Adventure Club

Want more fiction from Kari, including stories, discounts, and box sets not available anywhere else? Want to hear about locations, research, and other cool things that inspired this story and beyond? All that and adorable pet photos, too?

Join The Confidential Adventure Club and get a thank you gift of a free short story and a whole lot more at www.smarturl.it/c-a-club.

Hope to see you there!

**Novels:**

*Until Death*

*The Dream Thief*

*Dreaming the Storm: Book One of the Storms of Future Past Series*

*Joining the Storm: Book Two of the Storms of Future Past Series*

*Fighting the Storm: Book Four of the Storms of Future Past Series*

**Novellas:**

*Songs in the Mountain*

*Legacy of the Land*

*Restricted Species*

*In the Pines*

*Into the Storm: Book Three of the Storms of Future Past Series*

**Short Stories:**

*Renovations*

*Intentions*

*The Garbage Belt*

*The Seeds of Love*

*Wicked Bone*

*The Sound of Murder*

*Terminalia*

*Little Five: A Terminalia Story*

*Reflections*

**Collections:**

*Fantastic Women: A Dark Fantasy Novella Trio*

*Fantastic Shorts: Volume 1 - A Fantasy Short Story Collection*

"Kari Kilgore is an author to watch—her lyrical voice a siren song; her insight, conjured voodoo."

—Richard Thomas, author of *Breaker* and *Tribulations*